Run Masked

They are neighbours and friends, helping each other 'prove-up' their homesteads on time. There are plenty of others like them in Cannon Valley, except for the fact that the areas of land belonging to each of the men are coveted by someone who knows a secret that they don't. And that's when the trouble begins: framed for murder, both men start running with a 'shoot on sight' order ringing in their ears.

It becomes a case of run, run and run some more, and hope to out-run the bounty hunters' bullets.

Run Masked

Jake Douglas

A Black Horse Western

ROBERT HALE · LONDON

ISBN 978-0-7198-1816-5

Robert Hale Limited
Clerkenwell House
Clerkenwell Green
London EC1R 0HT

www.halebooks.com

Typeset by
Derek Doyle & Associates, Shaw Heath
Printed and bound in Great Britain by
CPI Antony Rowe, Chippenham and Eastbourne

PROLOGUE

MASKED MAN

The man on the wrong end of the gun slowly lifted his hands shoulder-high after, as instructed, dismounting to stand by his hard-blowing claybank – there were dark patches of sweat on almost all of its sleek body.

'You needn't've worn that bandanna. I ain't dumb, reckon I know who you are,' he told the masked man quietly.

The gunman's cool, pale-blue eyes above the bandanna settled on the other's face. 'Careful, *amigo* . . . if I thought you really meant that, I might be tempted to shoot you. A few bucks ain't worth dyin' over.'

'Why din' you pick on someone who can give you more money if you're after a stake? You know I never carry much. 'Course I could be wearing my well-stuffed money belt—'

'I ain't that lucky, friend! But it all comes down to time – it's shorter than my need for a getaway stake – so

5

sorry it has to be you, but hurry it along, or I *will* be forced to shoot and go through your pockets while you lie there bleeding.'

The man-at-bay – name of Jake Cash – ran a tongue over suddenly dry lips and cleared his throat. 'An' I thought we were friends.'

'Well, I admit I ain't shot any *friends* lately, but if I have to. . . .'

The gunman jerked his Colt and Cash stiffened, moved his hands in a *Wait*! gesture, sweat suddenly beading his deeply tanned, wary face. 'OK, OK! You know I must be joshin'—'

'I don't feel like laughin'! Now, no more delays, Jake! Try it again and you're a dead man. You think I'm bluffing, just open your mouth and gimme some smart-talk. They can put whatever you say on your tombstone.'

'*Hey!* I was bluffin' I said!' Cash practically yelled, frowning hard.

'Guessed that. "No cash on Cash!" But you're the only one around and I ain't got time to wait for someone in silk shirt and gold rings to come along. *Start shucking out what cash you have!*'

As Jake Cash quickly began to feel in his pockets, the masked man's Colt settled on a spot squarely in the middle of his chest. 'Move faster!'

'Gimme a chance!' Jake smiled faintly, adding quietly, 'Look, I really don't have much, though – gotta dig deep. . . .'

'Then *dig*! Now!'

Cash was mildly surprised at the tension in the other's tone. It usually took a lot to throw Brock Chase!

6

'How come you're doin' this? I mean, kinda drastic, for you, ain't it? What's happened up there in them hills where you. . . ?' He paused. 'Or was it something in town last night? Mebbe at Cold-Deck's, after I'd left?'

'All you need to know is – like I said, I'm desperate.' The cold eyes watched as Cash juggled some coins and a few low-value crumpled notes and tentatively held them out. 'Hell, you weren't kidding when you said you didn't have much cash on you. If you're holding-out on me I'll come back and blow your stupid head off . . . I mean it, Jake!'

Cash backed up a step thrusting the money towards the masked man. 'I'm not lying! I was at Cold-Deck's poker game last night: thought I seen you as I was leaving.' He nodded to the money as the gunman stuffed it into his shirt pocket. 'That's all I got left – sonuver deals from the bottom of the deck, you ask me.'

'Not any more.'

Cash stiffened, looked at the masked man quickly. 'You sayin'—?'

'What I said: just leave it at that.' The voice was ice-hard now. 'Judas! Is this really all you got?'

Cash made a placating gesture. 'Sorry.'

'That helps a helluva lot!'

'Didn't know I was gonna meet someone who needed a stake.'

'Don't push it! Just figure yourself lucky that you're able to walk away.'

'Jesus! Take it easy, Brock! You're really rattled, ain't you? What the hell's happened? Anythin' more I can do

7

to help?'

The masked man patted his pockets. 'You've done it – not enough, but I got no time to be choosy. Gonna have to take your hoss so you can't raise the alarm too early. I'll leave it someplace you can find it.' He gestured to a big clump of boulders on the rising slope. 'You can wait up there for a spell – someone oughta be along before sundown.'

'Most folk're home already, preparin' supper.'

'Lucky, ain't they?' Chase said, and patted his shirt pocket. 'Least, I can buy a cup of coffee now.' Then added with a touch of bitterness, 'And not a helluva lot more. Sure you've emptied your pockets?'

Cash said, spreading his arms. 'Welcome to pat me down, see for yourself.'

Those cold eyes above the bandanna mask crinkled slightly as if the man was smiling behind the cloth.

'Now, if you *really* knew me, you'd know I ain't *that* kinda fella.'

Cash chuckled after a few seconds when he realized what the other was talking about. He quipped, 'Well, I never was quite sure! Just as well you got a sense of humour . . . like stagin' this thing. It's to give me a kinda alibi for when Bronson pokes his nose in, ain't it? I reckon you're in big trouble, Brock. . . .'

The masked man grunted, but that was his only comment. Then he gestured with the gun, towards the west. 'Start walkin' – that way.'

'That takes me to hell-an'-gone away from my place!'

'Yeah, better start movin', or you won't get home before dark.'

8

Cash swore softly. 'How come you're doin' this to me? I never heard you was any kinda gunman or . . . robber . . . nor anythin' like it. Just a ham-an'-egger on a prove-up section, like me, and—'

'Things change, Jake. You play it smart – which shouldn't be too hard with someone like Bronson – and you won't be in any trouble. Now this is just for effect. . . .'

The Colt fired and the bullet kicked dust and gravel between Cash's dusty boots. He jumped, sucked in a sharp breath and threw the gunman a tight look before turning and starting to hurry towards the sundown fire.

'Now you can tell 'em I shot at you!'

Jake glanced back over his shoulder: the masked man was still standing there with the smoking gun in his hand. He raised his voice a little, 'Sorry for this, *amigo.*'

'The law'll likely expect me to tell 'em *somethin'* when they question me. They won't gimme a choice.'

'Just tell 'em what happened. Thanks for your help. If they do catch up with me, I hope I forget to mention that.'

'Hey! That's gratitude for you!'

'Called 'survival', Jake. You better get movin' . . . me, too!'

He turned and started to walk briskly towards some bushes, leading Cash's claybank.

'Hey!' Listen! Why run out! You've still got friends here'. Whatever kinda trouble you're in, you'll only make it worse if you run.'

'I'm *ridin'* out.'

'It's still runnin'!'

9

'Yeah, but—' A pause, and then three quiet words were spoken as the masked man disappeared into the heavy brush.

'I'll be back.'

CHAPTER 1

ON THE DODQE

The posse showed-up about an hour later, coming up the slope from a trail that could only lead out of the canyon where the masked man ran his small spread – the Lazy 'C', the letter, lying on its back, burned in with the brand.

Cash stood in the dying sunlight and waved. The heavily armed riders swung towards him.

The big sheriff, Carl Bronson, was in the lead and looked more sour than usual, eyes reddened, jaws stubbled.

'You seen him?' he barked, voice raspy from the dusty trail. His thick shoulders were hunched belligerently.

'Who?'

'Don't try that with me, Cash! Everyone knows you an' Brock Chase are friends!'

'Not . . . exactly.' Cash came down from his slope,

11

walking carefully in the loose soil. He stopped by the lawman's horse, the dripping sweat telling him it had been ridden mighty hard. 'We're neighbours, Brock an' me, but he's a ranny keeps to himself. Ain't nothin' social about him.'

'Quit that,' barked the sheriff. '*Have you seen him? I asked you!*'

Cash frowned, looking thoughtful. 'We-ell, I'd like to say a straight "yes" or "no", but—'

'You better say somethin' more'n you have so far,' growled the whip-lean deputy, Brady McBarr, easing in his mount beside the sheriff's, his narrow face set like granite – a very tough man, McBarr, and knowing it.

'Who the hell cares whether you're neighbours or not? Sheriff asked you a straight question an' wants a straight answer! *Have you seen Brock Chase?*'

Cash knew that McBarr had a reputation for playing it rough with prisoners: some said he had a year-round contract with the town's dentist for renewing missing teeth on prisoners he brought in.

Cash unconsciously touched a couple of fingers to his mouth, deliberately looking worried, and said, 'Well, I'm kinda rattled. See, *someone* just held me up and took all my money and it's shook me up a mite—'

'Oh, *someone* done that, did they?' the sheriff said sourly, eyes hot. 'I wonder who? All right, you got about two seconds to play it straight with me, Cash! *One! Two!* That's it! Brady, cuff him and put him in the cells for obstructin' justice.'

Cash frowned deeply, shocked: some of the posse afterward even swore they saw the white skin following

12

the blood draining from the man's face. Couldn't blame him, of course, not when it was McBarr who had charge of the cell block. . . .

'Look,' Cash said evenly, obviously making an effort. 'Mebbe I ain't thinkin' too straight—'

'Straight enough to describe this . . . *thief?*' demanded the sheriff.

'We-ll, he was wearin' a dark-blue bandanna mask so I didn't see his face. Held me up at gunpoint.'

'Took all your cash, huh?' McBarr asked slyly.

'I never have that much to carry round, Sheriff, just eighteen or twenty bucks. It's a lot to me.'

McBarr sneered, but the sheriff snapped, 'Duly noted! Now, you an' Chase've been neighbours for . . . how long? Four, five months. . . ? Yeah, about that, while you both prove-up. Seems to me, you *mightn't've* recognized him if he was masked by a bandanna, but *by Godfrey*, I know damn well, you'd've recognized his voice. Now, don't try to tell me different! All right?'

Cash was thinking fast: any good intentions he might've had of helping Brock Chase in some way went clear out the window at the sheriff's words – and McBarr moved in. *That sonuver really scared him.*

'I-I sort of guessed it *might* be him and – he took my bronc, by the way.'

'Or you *gave* it to him!' snapped McBarr. 'Which means you aided a damn fugitive. How you like dem apples, huh?'

'He just didn't want me to raise the alarm too early, he said. I din' mind him borrowin' my hoss.'

' "Raisin' the alarm" you says?' growled McBarr. 'The

hell you tryin' to kid?' He stepped forward abruptly and grabbed handfuls of the startled Cash's shirt. He dragged him in close, pushing his face right into Jake's 'Your real job was to delay us, wasn't it? Just like you're tryin' to do. Well, it ain't gonna work!'

The sheriff stooped down and suddenly interested himself in digging a small piece of crumbling gravel, no bigger than a pea, from under the shoe of the mount's left foot.

Other posse members suddenly found small chores to do as McBarr pulled Cash in close and rammed a hard knee up into the young man's crotch.

Cash gagged and doubled over. As he collapsed he vomited even before he writhed on the ground. McBarr stepped forward, raising his right boot, ready to kick, but the sheriff grunted, and signed for him to step back. McBarr looked like he might argue, but when his boss jutted his jaw – he stepped away.

The sheriff emptied a little canteen water over Cash's pain-contorted face, casually nudged him in the ribs as he leaned down a little.

'Where's you say Brock was goin'? Huh? Can't make out what you're mumblin' – just tell us where you met the son of a bitch and we'll figure it out from there.'

The suffering Cash nodded, gritting his teeth against his pain and asked 'It . . . it was right . . . here. But – wh-what the hell'd he . . . do?'

'Killed the sheriff's brother,' McBarr told him with a grim smile stretching his thin lips. ' 'magine some ranny bein' loco enough to do a thing like that! He might just as well've walked off a cliff an' saved us the trouble of huntin' him down . . . an', of course, anyone stupid enough to try 'n' help him. Well, you savvy, don't you, Cash?'

Jake moaned and was sick again, some splashing on one of McBarr's boots.

The deputy yelled, even shouldered the sheriff aside, and moved in on Jake, fists clenched and rising quickly from his sides.

Jake felt every blow jar through his body.

The sheriff concentrated on building an elaborate cigarette.

CHAPTER 2

'RUN, HIDE OR SHOOT!'

The man Brock Chase had shot and killed was none other than the infamous Cold-Deck – the gambler and cardsharp who ruled the roost in Cannon County where games-of-chance were concerned.

He *wasn't* the sheriff's brother, but his *brother-in-law* – black sheep of *Mrs* Bronson's family, and a mighty big embarrassment to her.

But it could also explain how a gambler-cardsharp with such a reputation for dishonesty was still able to travel Cannon County and set-up a game wherever he wanted – and always ride away with winnings . . . after the sheriff's share had been skimmed off the top.

Naturally, Cold-Deck had acquired quite a swagger, but he picked the wrong man to four-flush when he set his sights on Brock Chase.

Brock was a man who had been around: 'Living up to his name', as folk said, adding with a wink or a twist of the mouth to emphasize that Chase was not a man to tangle with.

Cold-Deck had been protected for a long, long time and was way past even arrogance. He had the notion he was untouchable simply because he was family to the local law . . . which fact he pushed to the limit. Sure, it dissuaded many a ranny with notions of arguing over the cards dealt him in a game with Cold-Deck, but once in a while someone did kick over the traces – and learned the hard way that the gambler had backed his nice-and-mostly-secure position by mastering the use of a hideout gun when it became necessary – *in his opinion.*

He had killed three men over the years – with long enough between-times for any new gamblers arriving to have either forgotten or to be ignorant of that fact . . . and gotten away with it.

But Cold-Deck, riding high that particular night, with a big win thanks to secretly marked cards, got a mite cocky and careless with Brock Chase: in from the hills with a small gold nugget he had found in a stream that crossed his land, hoping to build it into a stake that would allow him to shortcut his prove-up time with a cash settlement.

As Cold-Deck, whistling softly between his teeth, trying not to show his mounting interest in the gold, slid one of his hole-cards from the bottom of the deck, Chase, rubbing one eye that was growing blurred from long hours at the card table, spotted the move. He grabbed the startled gambler's wrist, twisting, causing

17

him to spill the whole deck which, later, admittedly, would have made it mighty hard for Brock Chase to substantiate his claim of cheating.

But it was quickly settled another way.

Cold-Deck made as if to scratch his neck, suddenly jerked his hand under his shirt towards the hideaway gun he carried. There was a loud explosion and the cardsharp was blown back across the table, spine arched, his shocked face now showing a third eye above his nose as he rolled off and thudded to the floor . . . dead.

One raking look around told Chase he didn't stand much chance here, not with this group of Cold-Deck's supporters. So he backed out with his smoking Colt and headed for the hills he knew best – and was lucky enough to run across young Jake Cash, who, he hoped, would give him a getaway stake.

In return, he tried to give the struggling young rancher a break by pulling up his bandanna over the bottom half of his face, then advised Jake, 'Just tell 'em a masked man held you up and stole your money.' It wasn't much, but at least it gave Jake some kind of defence: he could claim he was robbed by a masked man, identity unknown. *It might even work!*

Brock had always liked Jake: a hardy young rancher fighting the odds of weather and not-much-cash – despite his name. He was always willing to lend a hand at a moment's notice, too, would bring his own tools if he had the ones necessary for whatever the chore was.

He didn't like involving Jake at all, but didn't aim to sit around and wait for Sheriff Bronson to hang some charge on him for shooting his brother-in-law, either. It was no secret that the lawman was gradually working his way through the County, amassing land by trumped-up charges against current tenants so he could move in, foreclose, and claim it for himself, which he had already done several times.

Well, the shootout with Cold-Deck had been square enough and there had been too many witnesses for Bronson to claim otherwise. But that didn't stop the lawman from hassling Brock Chase, until finally he forced the rancher to go on the run, officially making him a wanted man Maybe the best thing now was for him to keep moving, Brock thought, clear the County completely, let the damn lawman have his hard-scrabble spread and . . . *oh, yeah*!

Not damn likely! He'd been kicked around most of his life, one way and another, and he had made up his mind that 'here' was where he would stay! *Right here!*

He was no fool. He knew the stranglehold Bronson had on the County, knew he was asking for more trouble than even the Devil himself could shake a stick at, but, by hell, it would take more than a crooked lawman to push him off his place in the Big Cat Hills, 'specially now he had found that small gold nugget.

Small was right, but it had rough edges, which meant it couldn't have been washed all that far downstream, and the stream – Catamount Creek – was mostly on his land, except that the upper section angled down fairly sharply from where it crossed the north-west corner of Jake Cash's place, higher up the slope than Chase's spread.

And which meant the gold's source was likely up there – somewhere, on Jake's land. But Jake was one man with whom he wouldn't mind sharing any further gold nuggets. He had cursed himself sleepless for using that small nugget in Cold-Deck's game, though. But, at the time, he had had the ever-hopeful gambler's conviction that he was about to hit a winning streak, so had taken the risk. But he hadn't pulled it off: all it had done was get a lot of questions asked about where he'd found the nugget, and were there more. . . ?

He felt he had fended the queries well enough, though: claiming he was tracking down a wolf that had snatched a couple of his calves and found the *lone* nugget – emphasis on the 'lone' – while he had been filling his coffee pot at a quiet backwater of the Independence River, well to the north of his spread. And Jake Cash's.

A little gold had been found in the Independence before, so his story likely had the ring of truth – especially when he made no mention of landmarks or other information that could help pin-down his collection point and he was trying to keep those things secret.

But Bronson's big nose had already sniffed out a possibility that Brock was holding back, so Chase knew he could expect more pressure soon enough. And he had played right smack into the lawman's hands by shooting it out with Cold-Deck and killing him.

Now he was Brock Chase, *fugitive*, on the run from whatever charge Bronson figured he could make stick.

No man in serious trouble with the law could own prove-up land, so Bronson could move in by his devious methods, take over, have one of his cronies work the Big Cat and, maybe to be sure about the gold nugget story, find some way to kick Jake Cash off *his* neighbouring section, too.

Everyone knew Catamount Creek watered both sections of land out there, and Brock's place was downstream.

Goddammit! He hadn't meant to lumber Jake with anything like this! he told himself for the hundredth time.

But, it was too late now.

Jake would be a target high on Bronson's list, just to be sure there was no worthwhile gold on Cash's holding that he could get his greedy hands on before, or maybe even *after*, the stream carried it down to Brock Chase's place.

Meantime, what could he do?

'You got a choice, you damn fool,' he told himself.

Yeah, some choice: *Run – hide – or stay, and shoot it out!*

There was really no choice.

Brock Chase wasn't the kind of man who would choose an easy way out of a sticky situation just to ease his conscience. No! It would have to be the 'right thing', or not at all. And the only 'right thing' he could think of here was to get young Jake away from the clutches of McBarr and Bronson.

Cash had already had a taste of what awaited him: McBarr's knee in the crotch. From what Brock could see from his hiding place among the trees above the posse, Jake was suffering, huddled up into a ball on the

21

ground, hands clasped tightly between his legs, bound to be feeling sick to his stomach after a cowardly kick like that.

Brock's jaw hardened: something else to rectify – in part, anyway – when he got his hands on McBarr.

And he would!

Tangling with that arrogant and sadistic bully had been a long time coming, and he was looking forward to it.

There seemed to be some sort of conference going on down there, he thought, as he carefully parted the bushes. There was a tight group surrounding the sheriff and McBarr and he figured they were deciding whether to go after him, or drag Jake back to town – and a jail cell – hoping Brock would make his plans to break Jake free.

'And you're right, if you only knew it, you son of a bitch!' he muttered and eased the small branches he was holding bent to one side, back into their original position.

But he had better wait until Jake's injury eased off a little: trying to run or even mount a horse with your *cojones* damaged would be no fun at all.

They were moving out!

It happened so suddenly that even though he was watching for the signs, he was more than a little surprised when they mounted abruptly and a couple of men started back in the direction of town.

But the rest – maybe eight men – stayed long enough to drape poor Jake, belly-down, over his horse, tying his wrists awkwardly to the saddle bow. It was a better position than straddling the mount, of course, but the jolting would guarantee that Jake would feel every pothole and jar on broken ground, each time like a lightning bolt searing through his body.

'I think I'm gonna kill you, McBarr,' Brock murmured. 'And mebbe you, too, Bronson. Not right now, I guess, though I'd sure like to, but you'll keep. Gettin' Jake free is more important.'

The sun had gone down now and the afterglow was fading quickly, which suited Brock.

He wasn't certain that Bronson would try to make it back to town because he couldn't possibly do it before dark. But it seemed that the sheriff was in one of his well-known 'bitch' moods and the group moved out, grumbling.

At first Brock thought they were just going to camp closer to the river, but McBarr led the way around the clump of granite known locally as Flapjack, because of its roundish shape and low height, and turned onto the trail to town.

Darkness would close in faster once the posse got in amongst the scattered timber, and that gave Brock his notion on how to get Jake away.

As he had surmised, after full dark came, there were complaints from the possemen about needing their supper and it was still a long ways to town, until, eventually, Bronson said, with a snarl, 'All *right*, you hungry bastards! We'll stop for grub, but if I don't get a full plate of sowbelly and beans with a decent cup of java, *my* cell block is gonna be crowded with a heap of fellers who suddenly found out it's a felony to disobey an officer of the law – *at any time*!'

'Judas, Sher'ff!' moaned one townsman. 'Why you have to be so damn – crabby!'

There were a few murmurs – low murmurs – of agreement as Sheriff Bronson said, 'Cos I'm a bachelor, an' I know some of you married men've been nagged into learnin' how to cook, and I've got a sudden fancy for sowbelly an' beans. Now don't tell me there ain't someone in this posse that don't carry the makin's of such a meal. . . ?'

Back in the trees, Brock smiled crookedly. 'That's it, Bronson. Be stupid! Stir 'em up an they won't give a good goddamn about stayin' awake on watch. Or followin' any other orders you give.'

And he was right.

The sour lawman picked and complained and put the men seconded to be the cooks into a ripe old mood of rebellion by the time the meal had been cooked and served.

'Now I aim to get me a decent sleep, seein' as that meal was, well, passable, I guess – *just*!' Bronson allowed, grudgingly, spreading his bedroll. 'We'll spend the night here now and the prisoner better be right where he is, hogtied to that log, when I wake up.'

There was a lot of murmuring over last cigarettes after Bronson finally turned in, and the man chosen for first guard duty settled in comfortably against the curving base of a cottonwood, head resting against the bark, already yawning.

Watching, belly growling a little at the lingering

odour of the posse's meal, Brock Chase eased his gun out of leather, crouching in the shadows well past the reach of the dying firelight.

No one had been given the job of keeping the fire alive for breakfast and it died away to a heap of glowing coals leaving the camp in almost total darkness.

Brock yawned his way through the next hour or so until the cacophony of snoring in the camp rivalled the sounds of insects and night creatures in the trees where he crouched stiffly.

He then picked out Jake's position, crept in slowly and carefully and lightly touched the prisoner's shoulder.

Jake's eyes snapped open. He looked straight up into Brock's rugged face, barely visible in the dying glow, and waited. He smiled slightly as he felt Brock's hands feeling for the ankle bonds – his hands were manacled – and then the brief touch of cold steel before the rope strands parted one by one.

'Legs're ... numb,' he gritted against Brock's ear. 'And I feel like a hoss stomped me.'

Chase nodded, then picked up the prisoner before he floundered and made a noise, rammed his shoulder into the man's midriff so he folded over his left shoulder with a small gasp of '*Judas – priest!*'

Then Chase made his way carefully through the snoring men – holding his breath – and headed for the trees.

Almost at the edge of the camp he stopped, breath catching in the back of his throat.

He could hear water running close by – not creek water or anywhere near as loud as that.

It was human water – someone urinating – and at that moment, he saw the man. Big and hulking in blurred outline against the trees, swearing softly as he fumbled while trying to button his fly.

His head turned and looked right at the frozen Brock.

'Musta been tha' extry jug o' cider, Ol' Greasy'd been hidin',' he slurred, swaying. 'How much you have? Hey! Wait up!' The man suddenly leaned closer. 'Whothehel'reyou?' he slurred, right hand now reaching back for his six gun – which wasn't there.

Likely he had taken it off before going to sleep and hadn't put it on again. But he was sobering fast and raised his voice. 'We got us a-a-a 'truder!' His voice cracked and the words were barely understandable. 'He's a . . . wha—'

'For Chris'sake go back to sleep, Howie! This is the third time you've woke me an' you do it again, I'll bend a brandin' iron over your thick skull!'

'Judas!' cried another sleep-edged voice. 'You're makin' more noise than Howie! Shut up the lotta you!'

Others were stirring now and Brock took a chance, swung at the swaying Howie and connected. As he had hoped, the man stumbled backward, tripping over someone stretched out in his blankets on the ground.

Foul language seared the night and it seemed to Brock that half the camp were awake now, all yelling and a few throwing their blankets aside.

He didn't waste any more time.

While the disturbance got louder and more profane, Brock carried Jake, who was shaking with barely contained laughter, into the safe darkness of the timber.

26

He was breathing hard by the time he had worked a short way into the trees and set Jake down against a rock. He wiped sweat from his forehead before it stung his eyes, glanced back at the distant camp. 'Lucky they've been boozing.'

'What a send-off, eh?' Laughter still edged Jake's voice as he sobered slowly. 'Ol' Bronson's gonna bust a gut when he finds out I've give him the slip.'

'We've still gotta get rid of them cuffs.'

'Uh-huh.' Jake was still chuckling, but tried to be serious. 'Get me a nail from somewhere and I'll soon do that.'

Brock frowned in the darkness. 'How would you know what to do?'

'Long story. We oughta pass Bill Winters' place on the way back. That old tumbledown line shack of his'll have some nails still holding a few timbers together. We can work one out that'll do the job.'

'You're full of surprises, Jake.'

'Surprise myself at times. Thanks for gettin' me away, Brock. I was scheduled for some mighty rough stuff.. They've got gold-fever now, the sonsabitches! Still, I would've liked just a few seconds more before we left.'

'Why, for hell's sake? We shaved it pretty fine as it was.'

'So I could've kicked McBarr in the *cojones*,' Jake said with feeling. 'Christ, I'm hurtin'! Even when I laugh.'

'If you'd done that, McBarr's screams would've woke the whole damn camp.'

'Yeah,' Jake allowed sorrowfully. 'Be like music to my ears!'

CHAPTER 3

NIGHT RUN

As good as his word, Jake Cash took the rusted, bent nail that Brock prised out of the weathered wood of the remains of Bill Winters' line shack, and worked with his back toward Brock for a few minutes. Then grinning, he turned and held up the dangling cuffs.

'*Da-da!*'

Brock inclined his head in acknowledgement. 'Mebbe I better not ask where you learned how to do that.'

'Wouldn't believe me if I told you.' Jake massaged his raw wrists. 'You got the makin's?'

Brock took his tobacco sack and papers from his shirt pocket and handed them to Jake who sat down in the grass at the edge of the stream they had come across.

He built a cigarette quickly and handed the makings back to Brock. 'We better get under cover if you need a smoke that bad,' Chase said.

Jake grunted and they moved into some rocks where they had ground-hitched the horses. Chase sat on a low rock, built and lit a cigarette himself, smoking it with his hand cupped around it – as Jake was now doing – helping disperse the smoke a little more, though a good tracker would rely as much on his sense of smell as his vision.

'What'd you mean when you said Bronson and McBarr had the gold fever?' Chase asked. 'There's always been a little gold found in this general area, hasn't there?'

'Uh-huh. That's because some folk keep lookin' for the bonanza – just won't give up. They look, find a little gold or none at all, drown their sorrows at the nearest bar, and someone else picks up on what they've been bitchin' about, sees gold nuggets big as your fist flashin' before his eyes, and heads for the hills. Finds a little more, mebbe, has to boast about it, naturally. Someone else hears and figures there just might be enough left for him and—' He shrugged. 'Way it goes . . . keeps the legend alive.'

Brock exhaled, looked at Jake through the smoke. 'But what you're sayin' kinda stretches things some, don't it?'

Jake smiled as he shook his head.

'You say that 'cause you dunno the full story.'

'I guess I don't. You'll have to tell me about this legend. I've heard it mentioned but not what it referred to.'

Jake yawned. 'OK. But I'm really beat now, Brock.' He looked around swiftly. 'S'pose we better find a

29

better place than this for the night – what you think?'

Brock looked mildly disappointed but nodded slowly.

'We're almost back at my spread here, the north boundary. I know a good spot, not far. Even in daylight it's not easy to find. Might have to share it with a couple of my steers, though, but they sleep light and'll warn us if anyone's pokin' around.'

'That's for me,' Jake said, grunting as he stood and stomped on his cigarette butt.

There were no cows using the grassy bench Brock took them to, but there was a rattlesnake, and Jake surprised the hell out of Chase by stomping on it, grinding the ugly head to mush under his right boot.

'Judas, man! That's damn risky! Mighta got your leg.'

'Keeps my reflexes honed. My old man used to catch 'em by grabbin' 'em behind the head with thumb and forefinger, then cutting the head off with his Bowie.'

'He live long?'

Jake grinned. 'Into his seventies.'

Still unsure, Brock asked, 'Die of snakebite?'

'Old age – an' pneumonia.' Jake was sober now. 'Tough ol' codger. Gave me a few wallopin's in his time.'

'We-ell, don't seem to've done you much harm.'

Jake Cash's face brightened. 'Comin' from you, that's – well, thanks, Brock.'

'Yeah, now, find yourself a snug corner, I'll take first watch.'

That brought Jake Cash back to reality and he drew his Colt and checked the loads, even took off his belt and counted the cartridges: the loops were two-thirds full.

Chase nodded approval and checked his own weapon.

'Ever shoot a man, Jake?' he asked quietly.

Jake paused as he was making a place to lie down. It seemed a long time before he answered. 'No, never wanted to.'

'That's good. Just remember, wantin' to and havin' to are different things – you need to decide quickly, and decide right.'

'I will . . . I *hope*!'

Me, too, allowed Brock silently.

Chase's theory had been that anything – or *anyone* – prowling around the bench would disturb the cattle which were sharing it with the fugitives and the nervous animals would, in turn, wake Jake and himself with stomping and low grunts of alarm, maybe even a bellow.

It worked – in one way – and also another way he hadn't thought of.

During the night, a strange horse whinnied down-slope – not loudly, just a protest for walking into a pothole probably – or even scaring-up another rat-tlesnake. The sleeping men – Brock was still doing his stint at guard duty but was half-dozing – awoke with a start: a couple of the steers were now bawling and stomping.

He shook his head violently to clear it, Colt in hand as he got quickly to his feet. '*Jake!*' he called in a loud whisper. 'Are you—?'

'I'm awake! What the hell—?'

'*Move!*' Brock hissed. 'They've found us – or will have, now the damn steers've started!'

The night rang with the bawling of wakening steers which in turn startled the fugitives' mounts, and they answered with shrill whinnies and stomping.

The horses hadn't been unsaddled, Brock figuring that was just a mite *too* risky, but they were securely ground-hitched and increased their noise as they tried to pull free. Brock was already releasing his own mount and Jake was only seconds behind freeing his horse.

They could hear men cursing downslope, and the clatter of hoofs as they tried to mount up in the dark, ready to come see what was disturbing the steers.

'Go!' Brock said emphatically, vaulting into leather. After a brief hesitation, he heard Jake's horse scrabbling at the part of the slope he had told him to use for a fast getaway. Chase triggered his six-gun, lying low over his mount's straining neck. The animal whickered in protest, jerked left – downhill.

Brock reared up in the saddle, yanking on the reins, fighting the now alarmed mount as it tried to reverse its move. He used his full weight to haul the straining head around and the hoofs scraped at the downslope, found loose gravel and . . . *he felt the horse going out under him.*

All he could do was go with it, kicking his boots free of the stirrups. 'Brock! You all—'

That was all he heard from Jake and then he was briefly flying through the air, jolting hard moments later, sliding, fighting for breath.

He had the rein ends wrapped about his left wrist and felt that arm jerk violently in its socket. Somehow he managed to hold on, but skidded as he was dragged, and the kicking, protesting animal threatened to slide on top of him.

Dammit! He couldn't get his wrist free of the reins! Above the rush of blood through his head he heard the crack of pistols, and the dull slap of a shotgun from downslope.

'Get outa here, Jake!' he called hoarsely, not even sure the younger man would hear him above the racket that had suddenly filled the night.

He threw his arms over his head for protection as wildly flailing hoofs threatened to brain him. One arm jolted and went numb – and he was thankful that, at least, it wasn't his gun-arm, but, *by Godfrey, it hurt*!

He was completely disoriented by now, still trying to protect himself from those whistling hoofs, feeling the hot, straining body still threatening to roll on top of him.

Then he felt himself slide into a shallow depression and knew instantly this *had* to be his one chance to escape the danger. He even had the less-than-serious thought that his name was 'Chase', wasn't it? So now was the time to live up to it: 'Chase your luck, if you have any left.'

One of his father's old sayings: 'Chase your luck, boy, it ain't gonna come to you.'

Long afterward, recalling those terrifying moments, he couldn't believe his mind had done that to him.

But now, he smothered the silly thoughts and

pressed himself down into the depression, realizing with a pleasant shock that finally, his arm was free from the restricting reins. Not that it felt much different: it was still numb and awkward to move even a few inches.

The night, already dark, now went even blacker than black as a tremendous weight momentarily crushed him into unyielding ground, but it eased abruptly before his ribs cracked. How they *didn't* snap he never did savvy, but something his mother used to say at such times flashed into his mind: 'Ours not to reason why, dear Brock. . . .'

Now he was busy squirming out of the depression as the horse rolled on over and then thrashed and whinnied as it tried to stop its slide downwards. On his knees, groggy and choking for breath, ribcage hurting, he staggered part-way upright, having to put down one hand to keep from falling flat again.

That was when Jake hauled his own nervous mount on to its haunches and yelled, 'Climb up behind!'

It was awkward, and the horse didn't co-operate well. Chase danced about beside it, muttering curses as he tried to get enough purchase so he could heave himself up.

Then Jake's hand closed under his half-numb arm and Brock instinctively grabbed at him, heaved with his shaky legs. Combined with Jake's efforts he floundered on to the horse's rump and somehow managed to get a leg either side moments before he hooked an arm about Jake's slim waist.

'Let's get the hell . . . outa . . . here,' he croaked.

'No argument with that!' grated Jake in response

and jammed in his heels.

Jake knew this part of Brock's spread as it bordered a short section of his own land. So they got underway quickly, the gunfire rattling but fading below.

'Stay this side of the line,' Brock yelled into his ear. 'I can pick up another mount down at my branding corrals – and a rifle.'

Jake only grunted and swung the straining mount a little more to the south of the line of trees. They heard voices yelling as the gunfire faded and Jake looked over his shoulder into Brock's sweating face.

'They're closer than I figured,' he said.

'Keep going! Turn left where the clump slants down. We can give 'em the slip that way – I hope.'

'A-men to that!'

CHAPTER 4

'DAMN POSSE!'

'Damn posse's *still* comin'!' Cash said, as his straining horse carried its double load up yet another slope, but they were well into Brock's land now. 'Can't see 'em though.'

'They're making one helluva noise; whoever's in charge ain't doing much to control 'em.'

Jake weaved the sweating mount up a little higher, eased it into a stand of scrubby trees where he hauled rein.

'Yeah,' Chase said approvingly. 'Mount needs a break.'

'Me, too,' Jake said, mopping his face and neck with his bandanna. Sharing a little water from Jake's canteen, they looked around, straining to see. 'Not enough starlight. Guess you know just where we are?'

'Heading a little south, takes us away from the ranch house, but that's all to the good – for now.'

'How's that? "*Good for now*?"'

The horse was blowing hard and Brock said to let it get its breath back before talking any more. He heard the puzzlement in Jake's query as if to say, Why do that?

'So we don't have to talk so damn loud to hear what we say,' Brock said in a strong whisper. 'They'll figure we came up the slope as the easiest way over here, but if we go quiet as we can now, we can get behind this scrub and there's shortcuts no one knows about but me that'll take us a long ways from here. They'll still be searchin' come daylight.'

'OK, but where we gonna go?'

'Coupla places in mind. Might just go back to the house and turn in for a spell.'

Jake started to haul rein instinctively, startled by Brock's words, but Chase urged him to keep going.

'You hit your head back there?' Cash asked softly.

There was a touch of a smile in Brock's voice as he said, 'No, but I hit just about everything else. Now, come on! Let's move.'

The posse wasn't giving up.

That much was clear even before they got behind the scrub where Brock directed Jake to a ridge hidden by the low growth of brush.

'Sonuvers want us bad,' Brock allowed, listening, straining to get a better view of where he figured the posse was.

'Want *somethin'* bad – not necessarily us,' Jake said, and Brock looked at him sharply, couldn't make out his expression in the bad light, but nodded slowly.

'Could be. What you got that Bronson or McBarr

would want?'

'Well, it ain't money! I ain't got enough of *that* left to interest that bunch, more likely to be you.'

Brock Chase thought about it briefly. 'There's the gold, of course, but not enough to stir 'em up.'

Jake was silent briefly, then said, quietly, 'Now there's where you could be wrong.'

Brock frowned, knowing Jake couldn't see the expression, but his puzzlement was obvious in his voice.

'You know somethin' I don't?'

'Might be. . . .' He let the last word drag out.

Then Brock snapped his fingers. 'This damn "legend" – thing you mentioned before, that it?'

'Yeah. It *is* only a legend, but – well, there always seems to be just enough to the stories to – not prove 'em, exactly, but enough to make it seem worthwhile to follow up and mebbe learn a little more about what happened.'

Brock waited, but Jake remained silent, obviously mulling over in his mind whatever information he had about the so-called 'legend'.

Chase grew impatient. 'It'll be daylight at this rate before I know any more, goddammit!'

Jake gave a mild start. 'Huh. . . ? Yeah, well, I was just figurin' whether it was worth tellin' you, or would I be wastin' your time.'

'*Our* time! All right. If you're serious about telling me now. . . .' He waited for Jake to nod, then grunt, to show he was serious. 'Let's get rid of this damn posse and then you can give me details over a cup of coffee.'

'Coffee? With them sonuvers out there with cocked guns?'

'Leave that part to me. First I'll want to know how much effort this *legend* is worth.'

His eyebrows arched as Jake chuckled. 'Oh you doubtin' Thomas. Are you in for a surprise. Come on. Let's go scare hell outa that posse first. . . .'

And that was just what they did.

With Brock showing the way in the dark, they twisted through more scrub, then suddenly came to a thin line of trees. As Jake reined down there were the sounds of restless cattle trying to sleep.

'The hell! Judas, you've led us right back to your herd. Where'd we take a wrong turnin'?'

'Haven't, this is where I was makin' for.' Chase had already jumped down from his uncomfortable position, rubbing his backside vigorously. 'I can pick up a spare mount down the far corner of the field, but I'll walk down.'

'And what do I do? Sit an' twiddle my thumbs?'

'You could tear up a couple them bushes right beside your hoss. I'll go across to the brandin' pen and collect a rifle I keep there with a few cans of food, and get back here in time to take some of the bushes from you.'

'I'm gonna be bustin' a gut while you wander around callin' up your bronc?'

'*Two* bushes is all we need, with a length of rope on each. . . .' Brock's voice was dwindling as he moved away.

He was back in several minutes, riding bareback on a sleek roan that was not all that happy about being woken up to find it had acquired a rider.

'And now. . . ?' panted Jake, breathless from struggling with the bushes.

'Now we tie a length of rope on each bush which we set on fire, then we tow one apiece down each side of where the herd's hunkered down and—'

'With you now,' cut in Jake. 'I hear that posse searchin' and ridin' back and forth the other side of the scrubline. We better move, huh? And *fast*!'

'That's it. Come on.'

The sight of burning bushes in the night drew some yells and several shots from the searching posse and they set their mounts after the fugitives, a couple shouting in excitement now as they figured they were closing in on their quarry.

Until the posse heard the sudden, startled bawling of disturbed cattle, followed quickly by the gathering thunder as the herd lunged through the night, already in stampede mode. . . .

The fugitives watched from a rise within the first line of trees that bordered the pasture. There was enough starlight for them to see – and enjoy! – the panic the thundering herd engendered in the now disrupted posse.

Panicky voices yelled, likely from volunteer riders who lived most of their lives in town, but who had figured a night ride with a posse might be . . . stimulating.

It sure stimulated *something* in them!

Curses mixed with nervous yells, a couple of guns stabbed daggers of flame through the night, followed swiftly by a deep voice shouting that the shooting was only making the stampede worse.

Horses milled. Several riders were thrown and there was one blood-chilling scream that wiped the smiles off the faces of Brock and Jake and stilled their rising laughter.

'Oh-oh,' Jake said slowly, but distinctly.

'Can't be helped,' said Brock Chase quietly. 'And we'd better get going while they're sorting themselves out here and finding each other. Just watch we don't run into someone who's panicked and liable to shoot at the first sound he hears, or shadow he sees.'

'Hell! I like the way you comfort a man! Where we goin' anyway?'

'How about that cup of coffee at my place?'

'You loco?'

'We won't be bothered by these *hombres* again tonight. You can count on that. We can pick up some grub, and spare clothes, and I've got a little ammo we'll no doubt need. This time when we hit the trail we'll be better prepared for the long haul.'

There was a short silence and then Jake said, 'You've done this before.'

'Mebbe. . . .'

'There's a helluva lot I don't know about you, ain't there, Brock?'

'Hey-eey! My life's an open book – just got a little fine print in it here'n'there, is all.'

Jake Cash shook his head slowly, smiling thinly.

'Let's get goin'. I think I'm startin' to feel kinda scared at whatever you're plannin' in that thing you use for a brain.'

'I'll hold your hand.'

41

Brock insisted that they wait a spell before they did any more to throw the posse.

'*Throw* 'em? You figure we can get rid of 'em?' Jake shook his head suddenly. 'Nah! We *might* throw 'em for a spell but these are *hombres* who live here. Been around for years, know this country like the backs of their hands.'

'Yeah, I figured that. It's why I took a couple weeks lookin' around these hills before taking out a claim for prove-up.'

'You done that?'

'Didn't you?'

Jake Cash blinked. 'We-ell, I mean, I looked at the country, rode the river to see where I could stake a claim that'd give me all the water I figured I'd ever need. . . .'

'There you are – that was the right thing to do.'

Yea-aah, but I din' look for any escape routes.' He paused, got no reply and added quietly, 'I didn't figure I'd ever need 'em.'

'Uh-huh. But you're already on the run – think about it.'

Another brief period of silence. 'Yeah. I get it now. You're on the run from somethin' else than just Bronson. Makin' sure you got a way out – just in case.'

Brock smiled faintly. 'Your brain's awake after all.'

'I don't reckon I better ask why.'

'We don't have time to go into that kinda thing. You coming now? Or do I go it alone?'

'You'd do that? Ride off and leave me?'

'You're free to choose. Just make up your mind and pronto.'

Jake frowned as Brock made it clear he was going.

'Hell! I'm with you,' Jake said hurriedly. 'I dunno nothin' about bein' on the dodge.'

'Then come and learn, but come *now*!'

'Hey! Wait for me! I'm comin'!'

CHAPTER 5

'KEEP RIDIN'!'

The posse was still trying to regroup.

That was Brock Chase's opinion. They were up high now, almost on top of a ridge that Jake had known was there but had no idea there was a way to the top from this part of the country.

'How – how long did it take you to find this damn snake of a trail up here?' Jake called, as Brock Chase led the way. They were on foot now, fighting reluctant mounts that wanted no part of the hang-by-your-nails type of trail they were following.

'Save your breath,' cautioned Chase, sounding a mite breathless himself. 'You're gonna need it. Just keep ridin'.'

'R-ridin'! My hoss's got blisters on his hoofs from walkin!'

'Save your goddam . . . breath!'

Jake closed his mouth, but had to open it again, to

44

pant. Brock sounded riled so mebbe he better keep quiet and just follow.

It was the best decision he could have made, though it didn't make the rugged climb any easier; in fact, seemed to make it longer, until he realized Chase was doubling back here and there without making it too apparent.

Slowly, sweat streaking his lean body, Jake Cash began to wonder just how seriously Brock Chase was on the run.

And what from!

Hell almighty. He might be tagging along with a-a murderer, or a bank robber or – well, who the hell knew?

Except Chase himself.

But, just the same, Jake tagged along.

Why? he wondered to himself. Just *why. . . ?* And he had a glimmer of an answer which kind of shook him: because he *trusted* the man. That shook him and puzzled him even more.

'Where the *hell* is the son of a bitch goin'?'

Far below, a ragged and complaining posse straggling behind, Sheriff Carl Bronson, took off his hat and blotted his sweat-streaming face with an already-sodden kerchief.

'Where the hell *is* he is a better question,' growled Deputy Brady McBarr sourly. 'Ain't seen him in an hour!'

Bronson snapped his head around and gave the big deputy a cold look, sliding his eyes back past the man's

45

shoulder to the few men remaining in the posse – some actually crawling up the steep slope, others dragging unco-operative mounts with straining reins over one shoulder on this rugged, dangerous slope.

'Judas! We gotta have this . . . bunch of old women along!' snapped the sheriff.

'You picked 'em back in town,' McBarr reminded him, and earned himself a muttered curse.

'An' we're *stuck* with 'em,' growled Bronson.

'You don' have to . . . be!' cried one of the leading townsmen, swaying on his feet, doubled over while he tried to get his breath. He lifted his head, the strain showing clearly on his haggard face.

'You don't have to be! Fact, you can count me out! Hell with you!' He waved a hand towards the wild country above, then let his arm fall listlessly. 'Them two ain't – ain't done nothin' for me to – to have a heart attack over. So, far as I'm concerned, Bronson, you can go *straight to Hell*!'

The man sat down abruptly, head on the forearm he now rested across his bent, shaking knees.

Immediately, the half-dozen posse men behind him, all from town, sat down and followed his example.

'Thanks a lot, *McNee*! *Thanks a helluva lot!*'

'Wel-welcome! An' still to hell with you!'

'Goddammit, Carl!' snapped Deputy McBarr. 'You gonna put up with this? I'll whip the bastards' asses up there!'

He was drawing out his heavy, rivet-studded belt through the loops when the sheriff stopped him.

'Leave it, Brady. I can't see any way across to that

mountain Chase is on. We'll all have to go back and try to find a way to take us up to where he is.'

'The sonver'll be in Canada by that time!' snapped McBarr.

'Then Canada can have 'em! I've had a bellyful. We'll go over the next hump an' if there's no easy way across to their slope, well, to hell with it! He ain't the only one figures it ain't worth a heart attack to get the bastards!'

Before he had finished, the possemen were wheeling their mounts and heading fast downslope, kicking up dust.

'Kerr-ist!' was McBarr's only comment, but he looked murderous.

'Come back here,' shouted the sheriff, but he was so short of breath, McBarr reckoned it sounded more like the bleating of a hungry calf.

He threw his battered hat on the ground in frustration and stomped on it – again and again.

Young Jake Cash was near exhausted, sat on a rock, head hanging, and then he looked at Brock Chase standing on a boulder, shading his eyes as he studied something beyond the peak.

'How the hell you know this trail was here?' Jake asked haltingly. 'You din't take up your – your section till after me an' I never knew about it.'

'I didn't arrive in town till after you, Jake, but I was up in these hills poking about for a couple weeks before I went down and registered for prove-up.'

Jake shook his head slowly. 'Question still stands:

47

how'd you know?'

'Just naturally cautious, Jake. Checked out a couple army maps before I came into this country—'

'How the hell you get your hands on army maps? Thought they was only for the military an' such?'

'We-ell, there was a kinda mix-up down in Fort Laramie one time, a kinda brawl between civilians and soldiers from the Fort. I got picked up with a bunch and I made a helluva fuss over mistaken identity. Kept it up 'til they finally put me in the commandant's office while he did some checkin' by telegraph. I amused myself by reading a brand new copy of some maps I found on his desk.'

'They – let you go?'

'Had to. Nothing to hold me on and they hadn't seen any new Wanted dodgers for weeks.' He paused and smiled. 'Likely still waiting for that issue to arrive.'

Jake blew out his cheeks. 'Judas! I reckon you're a mighty dangerous man, Brock Chase – if that's your name.'

'It is right now.' Brock smiled. 'I'm not dangerous, Jake, just not afraid to grab a chance when it comes my way.'

'Whatever the goddamn risk?'

Brock shrugged. 'If it's gonna save my neck now or later, I figure it's worth takin' a chance.'

After a short silence, Jake said, with a half-grin, 'Seein' as my neck's involved here, reckon I'll go along with that.'

'Let's get down off this peak and lose ourselves for a while – till the posse gets tired, leastways.'

'Sounds like a good idea to me.'

The next time Jake lost his breath badly enough to seriously consider what were the symptoms of suffocation, he changed his mind about the flight from the posse being such a good idea after all.

He flopped on to a rock, sweat stinging his eyes. They'd left the horses in a cleft, a couple of rocks pinning the reins. Seemed to Jake he could reach out and touch the clouds that seemed suspended so close. Frowning, he watched Brock build a cigarette and then proffer the tobacco sack. He shook his head.

'Brock, this ain't your land.' He watched Chase smile thinly. 'This – hell, we go much higher we'll come to the Pearly Gates.'

'Only if you take a *fall*, Jake. Higher the better.'

Jake was annoyed at the tone of Chase's voice – amused, even chiding.

'Dammit, Brock! *This still ain't your land.* An' well, I'd damn sure like to know where the hell we are.'

Brock lifted his right arm pointing, then sweeping it in a short arc. 'That hazy bluff you can just see through the trees? Recognize it?'

'Hell, I can't even make it out proper. Bluff? I seen it as we climbed, but I thought it was part of them cliffs near the trees. *Damnation*, it's the limit of my south line. Judas Priest! We must be high to see that far beyond the ridge!'

'You'll be sure of that when the sun goes down and your teeth start to chatter.'

'What? We gonna stay up here all night?'

'Most of it. We'll get moving just before sunrise and – if need be – we can be outa the area by full daylight.'

Jake frowned deeply. 'Just where the hell are we?'

'You know that tangle of canyons you can see from where you water your hosses . . . on your place?'

'Sure. I'm fightin' the critters all the time. Dunno what it is takes their interest, but they sure are eager to get back into them canyons.'

'All them young lady broncs, of course. There must be three, four hundred mustangs living in there.'

Jake let his shoulders slump. 'All right, you got me beat. But hell, you musta spent a damn long time explorin' these hills yourself.'

Their eyes met. After a pause, Chase said quietly, 'It's my way, Jake. Make sure I know where I can run to, if I have to . . . *and* where I can't.'

Then Jake Cash reached down for the tobacco sack resting on a rock and began to make a cigarette. Chase said nothing, looked around, moving from one high point to another until Jake had fired up and inhaled-exhaled the first few draws. Then he said quietly, 'Go ahead and ask, Jake.'

The younger man looked a mite surprised, but then nodded. 'Guess you know I have to, Brock. Well, *are* you on the dodge? I mean, all this checkin' out the country an'— I've seen you practisin' with your Colt, too. I say *seen* but damned if I ever actually seen you *draw*.' He shook his head once. 'Too damn fast for my eyes. Damn gun was just *there* banging away at your targets, an' hittin' every one. You got a lotta damn quick, Brock.'

'Comes in handy. But you gotta *keep* practisin'. Let

50

your speed drop just a breath and it could be too late.'

There was a brief silence and Brock was smiling faintly as Jake Cash snapped his head up and said, 'Well, dammit! – yes or no?'

'Thought I just answered that – or you did.'

Jake sighed, spread his hands. 'Yeah. I'm kinda dumb, I guess, but I knew there had to be *somethin'* with all that gunspeed. OK. I won't try to kid you I ain't interested in more details, but—'

'Wouldn't be human if you weren't, Jake. Mebbe I'll fill in the details sometime, but for now just settle for this: it was a long way from here, and it's a big bounty on my head . . . still claimable. There was a shootin' and I killed a couple people. One was a lawman.' As Jake's eyes widened, Brock lifted a hand. 'Not a good lawman, but he *was* wearing a badge when my bullet killed him so I'll be a hunted man till the day I die.'

'*Ju-das!* An' – an' you come way out here to this prove-up country to get away?'

'Here I am, Jake. There's your answer. Now we've got that off our chests, how about we make sure we stay well ahead of that damn posse?'

'Now, *that* sounds like a good idea.'

And Jake rode with that feeling – a *good* feeling, he decided – as he dragged his reluctant mount up another slope over steep broken ground.

'By hell, this – this better be worth it all,' he gasped.

'You're wastin' breath,' Brock told him curtly and, feeling his face flush at the rebuke, Jake nonetheless nodded and stayed silent as Chase led the way up and down and through twisting trails Jake decided he couldn't have found in a coon's age.

Then suddenly Brock Chase stopped dead, holding up a hand swiftly to forestall any queries from Jake.

But he couldn't hold in his curiosity for long.

'What. . . ?'

Brock jerked a head slightly forward and down.

'Flash of light.'

'Flash. . . ? Small stream down there – sun hittin' a wet rock, mebbe?'

Chase shook his head. 'More like the sun hitting the lenses of a pair of field-glasses.'

Chase motioned Jake to crouch down. 'And do it right now, where you stand. Try not to let your horse move.'

But, of course, there was a small patch of grass almost within reach and both mounts took a few steps towards it. Brock swore.

'Dammit! There it is again.'

'I see it! I see it,' Jake said, a little breathless. 'Someone sweepin' this area.'

'Has to be Bronson or McBarr. Not many range rannies'd carry a set of field-glasses taking up room for extra grub – or a whiskey bottle – in a saddle-bag.'

'They're holdin' steady. Right in line where we're standin'.'

'They're not that good. But I think they're sweeping this whole blamed slope.' Chase looked around, moving his head slowly so as not to make a point that might well bring the glasses to bear. 'Wait – *wait*! Just till the sun's not reflecting off them and then move smoothly as you can behind that row of bushes and drop flat. But keep a damn good hold on your bronc's reins. *Now! Quickly*, but no jerks or stumbles!'

They both made the move but Brock's own weary horse stumbled and, although he got the animal quickly behind the bush, there was a lot of scrabbling as the horse fought to get a firmer footing. Then it whickered loudly.

'That's done it!' Chase said tightly, steadying the snorting mount as it tossed its head.

A moment later something buzzed overhead, followed by several more sounds as clipped branches and leaves erupted. Then the delayed sound of the gun followed – a rifle, of course.

'Sons of bitches've got our range!' Jake Cash yelled, alarm clear in his startled voice.

'Must've been watching for a spell an' we only picked 'em up when the sun hit their lenses! OK, Jake! No point in playing pat-a-cake now – get into the saddle and *ride like hell*!

53

CHAPTER 6

HIGH CHASE

They soon realized that the sheriff – *and* most likely the whole damn posse – had located them some time before the sun flashing on the lenses of the field-glasses alerted them to this fact.

Chase led the way, Jake swallowing the dust kicked up by Brock's racing mount. It was apparent to Jake that Brock had done a lot of scouting around in these hills – and that likely was one reason why he was in real danger of falling behind in his prove-up deadline . . . yet, he continued looking for a fast, safe escape route.

Once again Jake wondered just what the hell this hard man had in his past.

The horse didn't hesitate as Brock gave it his signals and made a pleasing vision weaving and dodging and leaping over logs Jake had only seen at the last second, and almost came to grief once or twice.

But he followed Brock as closely as he dared and

almost died because of it.

Carl Bronson's men had been planted in mostly high positions that gave them the advantage of being able to half rise from their places, mostly without risk of being shot at as they fired, raking the trail the two fugitives were forced to follow below them.

'Brock! You all right?' Jake yelled, alarm in his voice as he saw Chase jerk and half-twist in the saddle. He thought the big man was going to topple from the horse and started to haul rein. But Brock merely hunched lower in the saddle, seemed to spin his body almost like a corkscrew and sent four fast, thundering shots up at a ridge where the bullet that had seared his shoulders came from.

Dirt erupted up there and a moment later there was a wild yell and a man's body dropped off the ledge, struck a jutting, narrow trail about six feet below and hung there with legs a'dangle as he tried to scramble back.

The sounds of his panicked voice reached them; 'Poley! *P-Poleyyyy!* Don' lemme fall, pard! *Hurry!*'

But Poley didn't seem in any hurry to expose himself and maybe stop the next bullet fired by the two fleeing men below.

'I-I better get help,' a new voice called, and Brock had no doubt it was 'Poley'.

'Yellerbelly!' he said, loud enough for Jake to hear.

'Geez! You frightened hell outa them!'

'Lucky I didn't shoot to kill, but not keen on shootin'-up normal folk dragged into a posse just because some local law says so.'

'Locals!' Jake said, still crouching, gun at the ready as he ran his eyes over the small drama above: the man up there managed to get a boot on the edge and drag himself to temporary safety, where he lay – no doubt breathing like a locomotive at his narrow escape.

Then Jake added, 'These ain't all townsmen, you know, Bronson's got some of his own hardcases in that posse. The sonuver you shot off that ledge is one.'

'So, you figure Bronson's bossing the whole deal?'

'Bet on it.'

Instead of answering, Brock Chase threw up his rifle to his shoulder and fired three fast shots. The rocky ledge where the scared man cringed crumbled under the concentrated strike of the lead and he yelled as he toppled after the collapsing rock and clay, bouncing down the steep slope to end in a part-somersault that left him upside down, almost standing on his head.

His wild yells had changed now to a low moan.

'You don't play a whole lot of that pat-a-cake you mentioned a while back, do you?' Jake said carefully.

'I always figure a man gets what he asks for sooner or later. C'mon, time for us to move.'

He dropped down the slope a ways and Jake, taken by surprise, slid and skidded after him.

Although they raised a good deal of dust, no one shot at them from above and they cleared the area without even a shouted curse to send them on their way . . . and it turned out to be an easy way at that.

But nightfall was a different matter.

Jake insisted he knew of a better, safer trail than the

precarious one that Brock wanted to follow.

'I've been here in daylight.' He gestured vaguely into the insect-humming darkness. 'Not this exact part of the range, but you can see the broken edge of a butte from here – see? It breaks across that line of stars a short way.'

'Got it.'

'Well, there's a kinda trystin' place there – er, you know?'

'I know if it's a trystin' place too many damn people will know about it, too.'

'Hell, no,' Jake sounded offended. 'Me an' Millie've kept it quiet for—'

'You haven't kept it quiet at all,' cut in Brock curtly. 'Use your head, Jake. Was Millie exclusive? To you I mean?'

'Yeah, of course! She wouldn't'—'

'She popular?' Brock broke in, and although he couldn't see Jake's face he knew it would be creased in a frown and maybe flushed in embarrassment.

'You bet! She's one of the most. . . .' His voice began to trail off. 'Aw, *hell! They line up* to take her out.'

Brock waited. He heard Jake sigh.

'Yeah, OK! I guess I kinda fooled myself she was exclusive to me like you said. It's possible she mighta gone there with another fella or two and. . . .' He paused, heaved a sigh. 'Guess we better look someplace else, huh?'

'Good idea. There was a dead-end canyon I came across one time I was scoutin' up here, a little ways sou'-east. Got a trickle of water coming out of the rocks. Be about as comfortable as a blacksmith's stockpile to sleep on, but that only makes it more appealing for us to use as our hideway for the night.'

'*Appealin'*? Speak for yourself!'

'Quit gripin' and let's check it out. We might get a night's sleep in before we *really* have to try to out-distance that damn posse tomorrow.'

'Sleep! Man, you got a mighty queer sense of humour, you know that, Brock? Mighty damn queer.'

'*Ha-ha-ha!* You comin'? I got a whole lot more laughs to keep you amused.'

He thought he heard Jake groan.

When Jake awoke in his blankets under a rock overhang, slowly as usual, mumbling about something he had been dreaming, he sat up groggily and scoured a hand down his face, blinking.

He coughed and turned his head to spit and that was when he saw Brock Chase's empty blankets on the far side of their small, banked night fire.

A ripple of apprehension passed through his body as he stood, using caution at the last moment as he grabbed for his gun. Turning his head this way and that, he swallowed and called softly, 'Brock? Brock?' No answer, so he made his query a little louder. 'Brock?'

Then he near died, he claimed later, when a gun barrel pressed against his spine and a hand clamped over his mouth at the same time as a soft, but harsh voice said in his ear, 'Why don't you climb up on that big boulder, cup your hands around your mouth and yell your damn head off!'

The words were spoken softly but angrily, and Jake felt his heart hammering as he twisted his head this way and that, trying to get away from that mouth-clamping hand.

He was finally released and he stepped away from the tall, dark silhouette and slapped a hand against his gun butt.

'You're a damn fool, boy! I've got a cocked gun pointed at your belly! You that tired of livin'?'

'You damn near scared me to death!'

Then a fist came out of the darkness and clipped him on the jaw, knocking Jake sprawling. Before he could squirm to a dazed, upright position, a boot slammed into his chest and pinned him to the ground.

He gulped. 'E-easy, Brock! I-I gotta breathe, man!'

'Could be debatable – and you'll stop breathin' next time you lift your voice above a whisper.'

Feeling alarm at last, Jake twisted his head this way and that. 'Th-they that close?' he whispered, hoarsely.

'I doubt it. Fact, I doubt they're even on this slope—'

'Then – then why the *hell'd* you—?'

Something in the set of the big man's shoulders made Jake cut off whatever else he was going to say.

Brock Chase's left arm suddenly shot out, circled Jake's head and pinned him against the big man's side. 'Quit strugglin'! *Now!* Better. I don't like sudden danger turnin' into no danger at all. *Why* would that posse suddenly abandon the chase? They had all the advantage – more men, more guns, more grub, spare mounts. Come daylight they could've run us into the ground, or picked us off with half-a-dozen good shots placed up

59

there on that ridge. You can't see it in this light but you must've noticed it before you turned in.'

'Er – aw, yeah sure. That ridge. Aw, yeah.'

Brock knew damn well the kid hadn't noticed it at all but let it go.

'OK. What I'm saying is they've got us outnumbered, enough men to sweep the slopes, but they've pulled out.'

'*Pulled out!* Why would they do that? They could likely ride us down before noon, like you were sayin'.'

Jake looked to Brock for an answer, but all the man said was, 'Think about it.'

'Hell, I dunno why they'd quit—'

'Mebbe they just want us to *think* they've quit.'

After a brief pause, Jake said, puzzlement in his voice, 'Well, if we did think so, we'd – we'd make a run for it deep into the hills, I guess, and why the hell would they want us to do that? I mean, if they wanted to set us up for ambush, they could do it right here.'

'Uh-huh. But mebbe they want us to just run. Go deep into the hills, follow the river out into Indian country, even circle round and come out the other side of town and – *keep* on running. Be a good chance of making it that way, but still unable to return to our prove-up sections being the wanted fugitives we now are.'

Jake was silent, suddenly sighed. 'You got somethin' worked out, ain't you? You got an idea of what this – this *schemozzle* is all about!'

'I dunno that I have, but it happened to me once before – don't matter when or where, same sort of

60

situation, aw, different set-up, but with the same thinkin', I reckon. I figured I'd outrun a posse that was half bounty-hunters and I made my run. Did it, too, got out from under.'

'And?'

He thought by the sound of Brock's voice that the man was smiling as he spoke. 'And then I found out – don't matter how – that some rich rancher who blamed me for maiming his son – which I hadn't, but could never prove it – anyway, this Rancher Galloway put up a big bounty on my head and he said he'd double it every two weeks I was still on the loose until I was caught and brought to him.'

Jake whistled through his teeth. 'Man! That – that musta got to be some bounty!'

'Over ten thousand before I realized the longer I stayed free that amount of money was bringing in every man who needed a stake and I'd have nowhere I could go without being recognized.'

'How'd you get away?'

'Did a little man-huntin' of my own and brought in the feller who did put the bullet in that rancher's son's back.'

'Did he admit that?'

'Eventually. But the point I'm making is, I was *allowed to stay free for a reason*. In that case it was just to let the reward mount up so eventually I'd have no place to go because so many would be after the money.'

Jake frowned.'What're you gettin' at now? You sayin' the posse after us is *lettin'* us stay free? I mean, why the hell would they do that? The reward on us couldn't be anythin' like the one you're talkin' about.'

'No. But I figure there could be some other reason for lettin' us stay on the loose.'

'What, for hell's sake?'

'As you're fond of saying, "a good question".'

'I mean, why would they want us to get away?' He shook his head violently. 'Don't make sense.'

'I got no answer to that and I could be wrong all along.'

'But you don't believe you are. . . ?'

There was a drawn-out silence when Brock said nothing and didn't move. Then he shook his head – just once.

'Only thing I can think of. . . .' He paused for so long that Jake Cash thought he wasn't going to continue. Then he said, 'Both of us are on prove-up, right? Means we gotta meet certain conditions to be eligible to work our land and keep it – long as we develop it to a certain standard within six months.'

'Ye-ah, that's right. But still don't see what—' Jake stopped abruptly, looked hard through the darkness at Brock. 'Unless . . . unless . . . by keepin' us on the run – fugitives, like you say – means we can't work our sections. We just *wouldn't be eligible if we broke the law*!'

'That's the notion I had.'

'But, why the hell? I mean, you an' me've got pretty good land – good water and graze, protection from the worst weather an' so on – but it's no better, mebbe not even as good, as some of the other land just north of the Bignose Hills. Why, up there, the blocks went almost overnight, they say, and they're a helluva lot better than ours.'

'Which means there just could be something we don't know about our land that interests some people like Bronson and McBarr. They don't strike me as bein' what you might call "reliable and honest" lawmen.'

'Hell, you got that right! But neither of them fought in the war: leastways not that I know of. I don't reckon either one'd qualify for a prove-up deal.'

'No, mebbe not. But they drive us off, we're finished. We can't ever get on that deal again, not once we're legally declared "fugitives from justice".'

His voice faded and Brock felt the younger man's gaze upon him as he suddenly blurted, 'There's somethin' there on our sections. Somethin' they want.'

'Mebbe it's time you gave me some more details of this so-called *legend* you told me about a while back . . . btut let's find a better place than this first.'

Jake nodded uncertainly. 'Yeah, but we got a posse of hardcases chasin' us, remember? And some locals who've lived here all their lives. We're practically strangers here, compared to them.'

'Then we better get movin', pronto.'

CHAPTER 7

'WANTED' - OR NOT?

Two days later brand new Wanted dodgers began to appear on trees and fences and walls all over that sou'-east area. They covered miles of country . . . and printed words were *BIG*, descriptions detailed.

Wanted for Murder and Escape from Legal Custody.
Approach with all due caution.
THESE MEN ARE DANGEROUS!

'Hell, we sure sound like a couple of mean despera-does,' commented Jake as they read together the dodger they had pulled from the trunk of a tree. 'But . . . murder? They could never prove that, could they? I mean, you gunnin' down Cold-Deck was all fair an' square – plenty of witnesses.'

'Witnesses who could be scared white by Bronson and McBarr if necessary,' allowed Brock. 'Make no mistake, Jake, Bronson could make the *murder* tag stick without even trying.'

'Well, how about me? I wasn't involved in that.'

'No, but you're a fugitive anyway. "Breaking out of legal custody" it says – that's enough to make sure you can never move back into the prove-up deal.'

Jake swore. 'Sonuver's got it sewed-up! But why?'

'I figured you were a mite sceptical about that so-called "legend" – me, too. But what if it *was* gospel? That the ore *did* end up somewhere on our adjoining sections?'

'I never did put too much faith in that story . . .' Jake admitted, but his words trailed off as he obviously gave some more thought to it. 'But – *by hell*, Brock! That damn ragged nugget you found! I figured, at first, it was likely from a small deposit on my land that got washed out, but. . . .' He paused, eyes widening some in a silent query.

Brock smiled thinly and nodded. 'Yeah, "*but*" . . . little word, with big hopes attached most times it's used.'

Jake's face lit up then just as quickly returned to its normal soberness. 'It'd be too good to be true if what we're thinkin' could be right.'

Brock Chase was standing on a rock to see over the brush that screened them and he shaded his eyes, looked carefully around the wild and rugged country where they now were. He took his time and Jake grew noticeably restless.

'Brock.'

Chase waved a hand to wait a little longer.

'Can't see anything, but they might just have a couple of men trailin' us to make sure we stay away. I reckon we've come far enough. Hell with 'em. If we want to go back to our sections, then why the hell not?'

'You loco?' Jake was shocked. '*Go back!* Ride into all them mean hardcases of Bronson's, just waitin' to see if we're gonna poke our noses in again?' He shook his head vigorously. 'Not me, *amigo!* Not *me!*'

Brock gave him a steady look, then pointed up the gravelly slope that rose above where they were crowded in behind some rocks. 'There's a big cluster of boulders up there. I reckon it has to have a clear area somewhere in the middle, and we'd have us a mighty good view in all directions. The loose gravel on the slope would cover our tracks so we wouldn't have to keep ridin' our broncs into the ground. We could sit things out up there for a while.'

'With that posse still lookin'?'

'But *are* they still looking? Most we've seen in the last day've been half-a-dozen riders down there, *supposedly* searching for our tracks, but they look to be half-asleep while doin' it. I reckon they're there to *be seen*, keeping us on the run, or at least away from our sections.'

Jake started to protest, frowned suddenly and then nodded. 'You could be right, you know. I-I had a notion, too, they didn't really seem to be tryin' . . . just there, on show to make us think Bronson's still after us.'

'Well, Bronson's there, all right, in the background, but while his men are making sure we see them still

66

coming behind us, *he* could be back at the spreads.'

'Our sections?'

'*Ours* no longer, Jake. They'll revert to Federal land now they've put us on the run – up for grabs, with us branded as outlaws. You can bet Bronson has spread the word we're on the dodge and so no longer qualify for prove-up.'

'And he's making it look as though he's guarding the spreads in case we do try to sneak back. If we do, he'll blow us to Kingdom Come and claim we were trespassin'.'

'That's if this *legend* story you told me *is* gospel.'

'I only told you what everyone's believed for years. No one's ever really proved it, but you comin' up with that jagged nugget— Even if it's only a possibility, I reckon it'll stir things up all over again.'

Brock was silent for a time then nodded slowly. 'I guess most of these stories of hidden riches are just that, stories someone's made up to fit the gossip. But. *There's that leetle word again! 'But,* once in a while they turn out to have some truth in them.' He looked around him and then sat down again on his rock and brought out the makings, beginning to build a cigarette. 'I figure we're OK here for a spell. Have a smoke and we'll go over that yarn you told me, the one about this legendary stash of gold that could've ended up on our sections.'

'Which ain't ours no longer, as you pointed out.'

'Just make sure you've got all the facts as you know 'em and we'll lay 'em out and take another look at 'em, right here and now. . . .'

There wasn't really much to the story, not as Jake had told Brock earlier, anyway.

He had noticed the sceptical look on Chase's face when he had finished and wasn't surprised when Brock asked, 'That's it?'

'Yep. But the story's persisted for a couple of years or more, now.'

'We-ell, let's see just what we've got here.'

It was simple enough.

At the time, there had been a gold discovery in the Bignose Hills at a place known as Fizzler Creek – the 'fizzler' part earned because someone had struck a wildcat seam with a couple of buckets of gold ore in it and had started a minor gold rush. But the 'yaller stuff' only trickled out in enough quantity to set the blood of hopefuls singing: in fact, the railroad even took a chance on it turning into a bonanza, and built a spur-track down to the nearby town in the foothills.

A shuttle was started specially to ship the ore from the main train at a whistle-stop down to the valley where the growing town was eagerly awaiting the boom it all promised.

But the Bignose Creek name was soon changed to Fizzler as the ore cut out without warning – simply stopped. One of those odd, apparently rich seams that often appear on the outskirts of a much more substantial deposit – raising high hopes, then stopping dead, leaving now useless prospecting pans and other gear rusting away in the sun.

Still, there had been a few small loads of ore before the crash-out and, as if presaging the slump that was to come, the spur-track gave way on its slope after heavy rain and the last load of ore tumbled down into raging waters that swept through the land and no real trace of it was ever found.

There was a lot of suspicion that the railroad men had been 'got at' by certain ruthless parties who paid them to arrange the tumble of the ore cars. Whether or not it was true, that particular load of gold was lost, and it was a fact that later the river changed course when part of the hills themselves collapsed into the valley. And *this* collapse formed the rich soil of land that would lay dormant all through the War years, neglected, until much later, when good, fertile land and graze were becoming rarer because of an increasing population. So that particular area became included in the government's prove-up project, designed to concentrate the clamouring, eager pioneers into an area of preferred development.

Then, two of those up-for-grabs sections had been chosen by Brock Chase and Jake Cash. When Brock brought in that small gold nugget with the rough edges, it started up conjecture all over again that the load of ore that disappeared with the train when the slope collapsed, more than likely was scattered about on one or both the prove-up sections.

There was no *real* reason to think so, but it was possible, and such a rumour refused to die. Oh, it wasn't mentioned for periods of time, but then someone wanting a free beer or whiskey would resurrect the old story and, with a wink here and there, hinted that there had been trace sightings of the odd nuggets that could well have spilled out of the original loads.

Brock Chase's small, raggedy nugget had hopes soaring that the legend had been true after all.

Now – *now* – Chase and Jake were both on the dodge of a kind that made them no longer eligible for prove-up, which didn't mean they couldn't claim any load of gold ore on what had once been their land, only that anyone else who located the legendary gold could also claim it. And if Brock and Jake were kept on the dodge, unable to return to what were once their spreads then anyone else interested could search there, too . . . but, if wise, would keep news of any successful recovery to themselves.

The value of the ore – though certainly exaggerated over the years – could still be considerable. And well worth the risk of being charged with 'trespassing on Federal land. . . .' for those trying to sniff it out: a crime which carried a long, harsh prison term.

Or, the trespassers could, quite legally, be *Shot On Sight.*

CHAPTER 8

'THIS LAND IS MINE!'

'There're men watchin' us from the brush!'

Jake sounded truly concerned as he brought this news to Brock Chase whose turn it was to do the cooking for the evening meal.

'Yeah. Noticed 'em a day or two ago.'

Jake frowned. 'You— An' you never said nothin'!'

Brock glanced up from ladling some of the stewed meat into Jake's bowl. 'You got eyes.'

'Hell! You've had me tendin' the damn hosses every coupla hours, fetchin' water from that spring up the roughest part of the slope—'

'Yeah, seen a coupla fellers up there, too. Figured you would've spotted 'em.'

Jake's jaw jutted as he clamped his teeth. 'I was too damn busy! Look, you shoulda told me! No! That's

71

what it boils down to – *you shoulda told me* you'd seen someone watchin'. Made *sure* I knew about it!'

Brock glanced at him soberly. 'You won't learn to stay alert if you gotta depend on someone else to look out for you.'

Jake frowned. 'Well, I mean, we're pards, ain't we? We should look out for each other.'

'Yeah, we should.'

Jake waited but Brock merely handed him the bowl of steaming stew. He took it slowly, sniffed.

'Wh-what kinda stew *is* this?'

'Best if you don't ask, but it won't kill you.'

'No, but what will it do?'

Brock looked annoyed and snapped, 'Eat it and find out! And quit all this gripin'. We got enough troubles without you bitchin' about the grub.'

Jake frowned again, ate a spoonful of stew and swallowed after chewing. 'Not – bad. I was just surprised it— Aw! Never mind. Er, how long you figure to stay here?'

'I sure don't figure to discover a load of gold that might've been buried at random four or five years ago in a couple of days.'

'That's what I mean, you figure it's really worth tryin' to follow through on that possibility?'

'Figure we'll never know if we don't try, and someone who knows this area a lot better'n us is keen to see us go – of our own accord – or be buried with a bullet or two in our hides. I'd say that *someone* knows the true odds better'n us.'

Jake's face reflected fleeting excitement, which he

made an obvious effort to cover. He cleared his throat and looked around, more casually than the moment needed. 'Got a helluva lot of ground to cover, Brock.'

Brock finished his stew before answering.

'Let's look at what we've got. A couple of sections of land, once registered to us as prove-up contenders, said to be at the foot of a slope carrying a railroad spur-track, now buried under that same slope.'

'Yeah! Half a damn mountain! How long you figure it'd take us to dig away all that dirt lookin' for a few gold nuggets? OK, OK! More'n a *few* I guess, but – hell, Brock!' He suddenly swept an arm around. 'Just *look* at the area of our sections. We could break our backs for the rest of our lives an' still not find that gold.'

'Could at that. But you're talking about looking for the gold itself, which don't have to be all that much, like you said earlier, but worth a lot of money. That's the way of gold.'

'Yeah,' Jake admitted with a nod. 'That's what I'm gettin' at. It won't be a big item to look for.'

Brock smiled thinly, shaking his head slowly. 'Me, I'm looking for something a lot bigger.'

'Listen! You said yourself there don't have ta be a huge amount of gold to make it worth our while—'

'And I still think so. It could be buried under tons of dirt and rocks—'

'Which'll make us old and grey before we find it—'

'Under tons of dirt and rocks, I said.' Brock let his words hang and Jake looked more puzzled than ever. 'But what else came down when the mountain collapsed?'

'Well, the spur-track, I guess, the small steam shuttle and its trucks. . . .' Jake's voice trailed off and he stared for a long moment, then blinked. 'Aw, *shoot*! That's what we look for! The damn spur-track or the shuttle an' it's cars. We find them and—' He suddenly looked gloomy again. 'But any gold ore would've been flung out and – well, it could be anywhere. Or no-damn-where.'

'But we'll have a *probable* area to work, instead of trying to move half a mountain range at random.'

'You really think we'll have a better chance of findin' it that way?'

Brock shrugged, sighed. 'I dunno, but seems to me we might and if anyone comes after us while we're looking, we'll see 'em from a long way off because we'll be a lot higher on the slopes.'

Jake thought about it, nodded slowly, but still did not look very elated. 'But it's still all guess-work, Brock. I mean, there ain't any *proof* that it happened the way they say, and if the gold *was* tossed out of a tumblin' train. . . . Man, we're drawin' a long bow.'

'Not a full-size *train*, Jake, a *shuttle* helluva lot smaller. Sure, it's still all wild rumours, but they've persisted for years so mebbe there's enough truth in the story to make it worth takin' a chance.'

'What about Bronson and McBarr?' Jake sounded dry-mouthed and ran a tongue over his lips.

'What about 'em? They're our problem whether we take time to look for the gold or not. It's gonna come to a showdown, one way or another . . . and probably soon.'

Jake licked his lips again, then nodded very slowly. He blew out his cheeks and simply said, '*Yeah*!'

He hesitated then, standing there, looking about him, and suddenly shrugged.

'What the hell, we don't try we'll never know, will we?'

'That's for sure, *amigo*. I hope your back's strong. Both our backs.'

CHAPTER 9

WORK FOR
YOUR PAY

It was a killer.

No matter how hard they tried, there was just no way of making things easier.

They did some fancy calculations which amounted to nothing and discarded that method while drinking gallons of strong coffee to help ease their headaches. They climbed all over the slopes, getting the sunlight slanting down on it from several directions. They studied the shadows, looking for differences in the colour of the soil – new on top of old. The theory was OK, but put into practice, it was not so easy to discern the contrasting colours.

They had to be on the lookout, too, for spies or maybe someone who figured they had more to gain by putting them under their guns.

When the sun went down, twice they kept working through the afterglow until it deepened too far into night.

It was hard, hard work – for no reward. Then. . . .

Savagely, Jake drove his pick deep into the ground and, gasping as he wiped sweat out of his eyes, said, '*Hell* with it! I don't think I wanna be rich after all.'

He flopped wearily on the ground. Brock looked up from prising out a clod of earth, kicked at it to make sure there were no signs of gold there, then picked up the largest hunk and tossed it away downslope. He dusted off his hands and started to speak when he suddenly paused.

'You hear that?' he asked, in a hoarse voice.

'What? All I heard was you cussin' a hunka dirt and – a *clunk*!' He sucked in a sharp breath. '*Judas Priest*! A stone in that lump hittin' – metal!'

Brock Chase was already moving across the slope, slipping and sliding, but coming up to the area where the clump of gravel-loaded dirt had landed.

There wasn't much to see, just scattered dirt, a handful of gravel, one or two larger stones – one of which had rolled onto the rusted end of something poking up a few inches above ground level.

'Jake.' Brock's voice was calm – *too calm*! – as he asked 'You ever seen a piece of iron like this?'

Jake was down on his knees now, examining the find.

'No,' he said, in a voice that was little above a whisper. 'Not *exactly*, but it looks a lot like the end of a mangled rail-track, only not quite so heavy.'

'Yeah, it's a little lighter, more like what they'd set on

a siding where it didn't have to take the full weight of a line of freight cars – just one or two.'

'Like a-a spur-track!' Jake said elatedly. '*Jesus, Brock! We're on the right spot!*'

'Mebbe, but don't shout, OK? We don't have to let the whole damn County know.'

'Well! Long as *we* know! I guess that's what matters.'

'It does. But we've got a helluva lot of work ahead of us. This is only a part of a spur-track and it's been here a long time. Might not even be the one we hope it is.' He stepped back, tilted his head and placed his hands on his hips. 'Mighty big mountain from where I'm standin'.'

'We knew that all along. Just never expected to get lucky so soon.'

'Mebbe it's lucky, but luck always comes at a price, Jake. Just think about it: a whole damn slope collapsed; this bit of spur track has been in the weather for a long time and it'll be well buried, mightn't even be the one we want. There could be a dozen more under there.' He gestured to the slope with all its imperfections, any one of which could be hiding what they sought. 'And we'll have to check 'em all – one by one.'

'Goddammit. Don't be such a wet blanket.'

'Well, you got some kinda magic wand you haven't told me about? No. . . ? Then grab the damn pick and *start diggin'*! Wishin' and dreamin' won't put that gold in our pockets.'

Jake swore, his eyes hot, lips stretched thin as he watched Brock Chase move a little way across the slope along the suspected line of the visible piece of spur-track.

Brock started digging, driving his pick blade deep each time, sweat-sheened veins and muscles standing out on arms, shoulders and torso.

Each breath gusted like a horse that had just run a mile uphill and Jake suddenly felt ashamed, realizing just how much effort Brock was putting into it, showing *him* by demonstration that any riches forthcoming were not just going to appear for the collecting: they were going to have to work for them, and work damned hard at that.

Jake ducked his head, took up his own pick and cleared his throat as he asked, 'Where you reckon I should start?'

Shaking sweat out of his eyes as he looked up, Brock nodded toward a part of the slope just ahead and slightly below where he was working.

'But not too close, or I'll be shakin' you off the end of my pick.'

Jake moved a short distance away and started swinging, punctuating his words with each driving blow of the pick as he said, 'Well, if it happens, bury me with a-a gold nugget clasped in my hot little hands, folded neatly across my chest. OK?'

'Not, OK! I'm lean an' mean an' hungry for gold, pardner. Now get goin' an' dig me a bucketful.'

Jake grinned and started to laugh but a cold-edged voice stopped him dead.

'Not on my land, you damn thieves!'

And suddenly a young woman in range clothes was standing on a rock above them covering them both with the double-barrelled shotgun she held, the hammers cocked.

The sun glinted off the blued steel as she jerked the weapon, ordering them to raise their hands.

She had shoulder-length, light-brown hair, an oval face – or nearly-so: the chin was just a mite too sharp to hold the promised symmetry. As near as Brock could tell, her eyes were some kind of blue – a little on the dark side, in this light, very steady, the pointed jaw firm and determined.

'Damn you! Are you dumb?' The gun barrels jerked again. 'Get your hands up! Higher! Now keep them there till I tell you different!'

'Judas!' Jake said, glancing at Brock who was raising his hands slowly but as directed.

'*You!* Kid!' the girl snapped. 'Get your hands *up*! And right this second!'

Jake's eyes widened briefly as he thrust his hands high, immediately feeling foolish – and not a little angry – at himself. But that shotgun looked mighty menacing.

She stood there, alert, eyes flicking from one to the other. She nodded at Brock. 'You, you're the eldest so you'd be – Brock Chase?'

'And you'd be Louisa Partridge,' Brock countered and Jake looked at him, surprised. Brock caught his eye. 'She owns the L-Bar-P.'

'But that's way north of here! Big as a—'

Brock nodded, giving the girl a questioning look.

'I'm expanding. My husband was killed by a wild horse some time back and his insurance—' She stopped abruptly and Brock clearly saw the self-anger drain the blood from her face. 'That's none of your business! This land is mine and you're trespassing. I'd be quite within my rights to pull both triggers.'

She moved the shotgun menacingly and Brock heard Jake suck in a sharp breath.

'Relax, Jake, she won't shoot.'

Jake frowned, mighty uncomfortable. 'You can't be sure of that.'

'No,' Brock admitted slowly. 'But what would she have to gain?'

'Trespassers get shot every day,' the girl snapped and Brock nodded, half-smiling.

'Not by someone who's ambitious, wants to spread her wings and knows she'll have to do it all nice and legal without any trouble with the law. Like having to explain why she shot down a couple of—'

'*Fugitives?*' Louisa cut in sharply. 'Is that what you were going to say, Mr Chase? Because I think that would be a more than acceptable excuse according to all those Wanted dodgers.'

Brock compressed his lips and then gave her a single jerk of his head. 'Thought you mightn't know about our problem,' he admitted haltingly. 'But it ain't true what Bronson's spreading around.'

He prepared himself for her scathing disbelief.

But she surprised them both by nodding. 'No, I don't believe it is. My foreman was there when you shot that dreadful – *thing*! – who called himself Cold-Deck. My man said it was all fair and square—' She paused abruptly and seemed to reach some sort of decision. 'Perhaps I was a little hasty in threatening you, but this

81

is my land now. And whatever's on it, *in* it or *under* it is mine.'

Jake looked quickly at Brock.

'Can't argue with that, Jake. If the lady's really bought and paid for this land, then – well, I guess we're trespassing.' He touched a hand to hatbrim, noting how her grip on the shotgun tightened. With just a suggestion of a smile touching his lips, eyes steady on Louisa, he said, 'Our apologies, ma'am. Now, if you got no objections, I guess we'll just mosey along and go about our business.'

The shotgun didn't waver and Brock could see the tension in Jake's stiff shoulders.

'That would be the best thing but you both look like you could do with a good meal. Why don't you come back to my ranch? I have an excellent cook, a French woman – a one-time . . . er . . . lady of the night who decided she would rather spend her life doing something she really enjoyed, cooking. Apparently her family were famous for their culinary talents in France—' She stopped and Brock swore she blushed. 'Oh! There I go, running off at the mouth again. But I do have a soft spot for – well, folk who get the wrong end of the stick through no fault of their own.' Those dark-blue eyes lifted to Brock's deadpan face. 'I come from a long line of battlers and I feel for other people I see struggling against odds that were not of their making and. . . . Well, I'm taking a chance on you two. You, at least, have a good reputation around here, Mr Chase. . . .'

She let her voice drift off. Brock's face was unreadable,

but there was plenty of turmoil in his mind as he tried to savvy this rather plain, thirtyish woman with the unmistakable mark of the outdoors in both her looks and manner . . . and the comfortable way she held that shotgun.

'Officially, we're still fugitives, Mrs Partridge, according to the law.' He shrugged. 'Whatever your plans, they could all be turned on their heads if you help us in any way.'

'That's the very thing I hate! "Guilty Without Proof"!' My husband was a man like that. He was blamed for taking part in a bullion robbery, simply because he *gave* one of the robbers – a man who'd saved his life during the war – a pair of boots because the ones he was wearing were falling off. They took all his entitlements as a decorated officer so that when he died they refused to pay me any of the compensation he should've been due.' There was a small tremor in her voice now.

'Didn't think they could do that,' Brock allowed.

'If you have an enemy in a position to arrange such a thing, it can be done.' She paused, adding quietly, 'And it was.'

She glared defiantly and Brock nodded slowly.

'Sorry to hear that. I guess that's why you claim any of the gold supposed to be buried here.' His voice slowed. 'Rightfully enough after you've bought it, of course.' He paused briefly, but when she said nothing, went on, 'We were just . . . er . . . what's up?'

Her mouth was tight and her knuckles were white where she gripped the shotgun.

'From what I've just said you know damn' well I

haven't bought this place. I'd *intended* to use some of the compensation I thought I was due to search for the gold that's supposed to be buried here, but I—' She shrugged. 'Well, with the way my luck's been running lately, I suppose it would have been futile, anyway.'

Her not quite hidden despondency touched something in Brock Chase.

'Don't worry about it, ma'am. We can all search together – if you've no objections?' She merely stared and he added, 'We'll split even-Steven. You have our words on that.'

He glanced at Jake who nodded solemnly. 'That's gospel, ma'am.'

She frowned. 'After I've just threatened you. . . ?'

'Ma'am . . . it—'

'Louisa, for Heaven's sake! Or Lou if you like.'

He nodded. 'Uh-huh. Well, we feel we've been hard done by, too. Framed for murder and such, put on the run so we're no longer eligible for our prove-up land – land that someone has their eye on. You don't have to believe it, but if your foreman saw me shoot Cold-Deck, then he knows this whole thing is a frame-up to get us off the sections we were workin'.'

'But why?' she asked and there was more care in those short words than Brock expected, or could savvy.

'Because legend' – he jerked his head towards the silent, closely listening Jake – 'accordin' to young Jake there, has it that there's a fortune in gold somewhere on this land. But you already know about that, don't you?'

Her eyes held to his face for a long moment and he

began to frown, when she said quietly, 'Yes. Jim, my late husband was somehow connected with someone who knew about that *legendary* missing fortune in gold. Some kin, or someone he fought alongside during the war, I'm not sure.' She flushed. 'And when they wouldn't pay me the compensation for Jim's death, I-I recalled him telling me about that gold, always insisting that it wasn't just some imaginary thing, but that it really was buried around here. I believe he meant on the land you were trying to prove-up on.' Her face suddenly sharpened. 'He was quite miffed that he wasn't able to look for that gold because of you,' Her voice quietened, as she added, 'We were losing money on the ranch, you see. Oh, it's big, all right, but our water is drying up for some reason, so our graze is poorly.'

He nodded. 'Figured it might be when I saw all them ups an' downs on your main pasture. Too steep. Water doesn't have a chance to feed the grass before it flows on. You need a dam.'

'We didn't know much about that kind of thing when we first bought the spread.' With a touch of bitterness, she added, 'We found out the hard way why it had been such a bargain.'

'You done well to last as long as you have. Sorry to hear about your husband . . . must be hard for you now.'

He thought her eyes glinted briefly and she made a show of waving away a fly that neither Jake nor Brock could see. Then she tilted her head up slightly.

'I'll manage!' Her tone was sharp but she suddenly added more reasonably, 'You know, Brock Chase, if we

. . . each pooled our knowledge, we just might find that gold.'

'Wonder why I never thought of that?' he asked, starting to smile.

And she slowly lowered the shotgun.

CHAPTER 10

NOT SO EASY!

It seemed like a good idea: neighbours pitching in together, each with the same goal, even neighbours not on the best of terms.

Find that legendary ore, long ago stolen from thieves by other thieves. . . .

Brock had a twinge of conscience – a *small* one. When you got right down to it, this, what they were planning, could also be classed as theft.

But there were plenty of others after the same thing so it all boiled down to first come, first served. He didn't try to fool himself: that was no real answer. But if the gold had been lost for so many years. . . .

'The hell with it,' he decided. The land – and what-ever went with it – would have belonged to him, anyway: after prove-up, sure, but he hadn't been given a decent chance to accomplish that. Still, he wasn't the kind to stand aside and let someone wipe their boots on him and then look for what he was rapidly deciding he had every damn right to. Him and Jake.

But – *but* – that Partridge woman. . . .

He sensed the stubborness in her, bordering on ruthlessness, if his instincts were anywhere near as right as they should be. It didn't mean she was dishonest, but she seemed mighty touchy, not without reason, he admitted, and there was a deal of worry there that she couldn't quite cover up.

He knew he would be watched like a hawk by her men, visible or not, and, possibly, by herself.

He decided she was an opportunist, which was OK, he reckoned: you didn't go far these days without grabbing chances when you could. It really only remained now to see if she was an honest opportunist.

He tried talking it over with Jake but the younger man was somewhat smitten by her, not only because she was a woman and was due some natural respect, but a handsome one at that. And like all of her species, she sensed this immediately, and threw plenty of smiles and encouraging words his way just in case she should need an ally, later on.

The two men from her crew she had sent across to help – and to watch out for her interests, of course – were good enough workers, but there was a hardness about them that seemed beyond that of the usual hired cowhand.

Specially the tall, swarthy one who called himself Chip Lang. He looked mean, wore two guns, low-slung, and seemed to watch Brock mighty closely: his almost total uninterest in Jake actually peeved the young man.

'If he didn't look so damn mean, I'd feel like callin' him out, the way he looks at me, like I ain't even there,' Jake complained.

'Don't do it, Jake,' Brock warned. 'I think his real name's Carver. Pretty sure I seen him in Laredo one time, shot it out with three men in the town square.'

'Judas! He walked away from that?'

'Killed 'em all and never missed a draw on his cigarette. Just steer clear of him, Jake.'

Jake had sobered now and, a few minutes later asked Brock, 'What's that gal doin' hiring a hardcase like him?'

Brock straightened his aching back with a grunt and dumped another spadeful of dirt on the growing pile.

'A good question, Jake, but I got no answer for you. Just do like I say: keep clear of him.'

'What about his sidekick? That dummy, nearly always close by him. He seems, I dunno, like he's sleepwalkin'.'

Brock smiled crookedly and winked.

'The hell does that mean?' Jake asked testily.

'Never judge a book by—'

'Aw, I know about that hogwash. But he hardly speaks! And he don't even pack a gun.'

Brock's face was sober now. 'Knife man. Keeps one up high behind his shirt collar. Calls himself Blade. Just watch if he starts scratchin' his ear or neck.'

Jake swallowed. 'What the hell we into here, *amigo*?'

'Unfortunately, pard, there's only one way to find out. Wait 'n' see.'

Later that same day, Brock looked around him as he used his neckerchief to wipe sweat from his face.

They weren't making a lot of progress with the digging. Muscles were aching and there sure did seem to be one hell of a lot of dirt to shift, and even then they might not be anywhere near the gold – *if* it was there at all.

The doubt had been creeping in for some time now but he saw Chip Lang looking at him several times, the man not using his pick and spade very enegetically.

'You got somethin' to say to me?' Lang asked sharply as he caught Brock watching him, one time.

'Nope.'

'Then quit starin' at me!'

'Mister, I've got plenty to keep me from lookin' at you.' He indicated a grey-brown lizard sunning on a rock. 'And better things at that, but I did notice you ain't worked up much of a sweat.'

He regretted saying it instantly, knew it was a mistake: he had let his feelings get the better of him. And the way Chip Lang smiled, Brock knew this was just what the man had been hoping for: a confrontation.

'I don't mind sweatin', and in about one minute I'm gonna work up a good one – after I finish with you!'

Brock hadn't thought the inevitable fight would happen so quickly.

But Lang didn't hesitate, was actually moving in on Brock even as he spoke. Brock started to straighten but the man had a handful of dirt ready and flung it at his head. He ducked but small stones and clods of dirt still hit him as he moved swiftly to one side.

Then Lang's body collided with him and knocked him sprawling, scrabbling on the ground which fell away steeply at this point. Brock slid wildly on his back and next thing he saw Lang's airborne body dropping towards him, the man holding both legs stiffly before him, big boots with their high heels and spurs ready to rip into flesh and bone.

Brock spun swiftly but one of the boots still sliced across his ribs, tearing his shirt and skin. He grunted, stopped his spin, and rolled back towards Lang. It caught the man unawares: he tried to stop in his tracks, but Brock's body hit him below the knees and he staggered, waving his arms wildly, trying to stay upright.

Too late! He was well past the point of balance and he stumbled, putting down one hand to keep from falling all the way. Brock kicked the arm away and Lang grunted as he dropped face first on to the rough ground.

Before he could make an effort to stand again, Brock kicked him in the side and Lang spun away. He flopped over on to his back and as Brock moved in, flung another handful of gravel squarely into Brock's face.

He staggered back, clawing at his eyes which were stinging with gritty dust, stumbling in his half-blindness. Lang chuckled as he closed, swung a hard fist against the side of Brock's head and drove the man to his knees. He took two long steps and rammed a knee up into Brock's bloody face. Brock flew backwards, arms flailing, head ringing. He hit the rough ground hard, feeling stones biting into his arms and torso. Then one of Lang's dirty boots caught him in the side of the neck and he was sure his head had detached from his body.

He didn't remember falling on his face, but the pain

91

of those heavy boots slamming against his ribs and shoulders was something that would remind him of these agonizing moments for a long time to come.

Lang danced around him, kicking him at will, wherever there was an opening or, if there wasn't easy access, he made it by wrenching a protecting arm aside, or grabbing Brock's long hair, yanking and twisting painfully sending him skidding across the slope.

Jake had made several attempts to step in between the fighters and push Brock out of reach of Lang's murderous fists and boots. He reckoned Brock would welcome even a few seconds' relief.

But Lang rammed into him with a driving shoulder.

'Get outa my way, kid, or I'll fix it so you'll never be able to father children!' grated Lang sweatily.

Jake swallowed and looked really worried, turned away and, as Lang sneered, suddenly came spinning back with the weight of his lean, moving body behind the fist he drove into Lang's midriff. The man gagged, surprised, locking both arms across his suffering body. Jake almost casually spread his hand over that bloody, contorted face and shoved violently.

Chip Lang went down as if a log had fallen on him. He lay gasping and moaning in the dust as Jake helped Brock dazedly to his feet.

'J-Jake, I bet Lang wishes you hadn't done that an' so do I!' Jake arched puzzled eyebrows as Brock added, 'I've got to finish this now, or sometime later I mightn't be quick enough to dodge a bullet in the back.'

'Hell, Brock, he used every dirty damn trick he could think of—'

'That's the way his kind are Jake, I 'preciate your help, but *I* have to be the one to finish this – OK?'

A little unsteadily, Brock stooped over the semi-conscious Lang and dragged him down the slope. The man was starting to come round, kicking, cussing, flailing his arms. Brock stopped by a tree with a large trunk, fisted up the front of the torn, bloody shirt and heaved the man upright. He slammed him back against the tree with an explosive grunt of effort. Lang's head rapped the rough bark and he slurred a filthy epithet, only half-conscious.

Brock grinned, showing blood-smeared teeth.

'Glad you're joining us again, Lang. Want you to hear somethin' I'm gonna say. . . .'

More than a little dizzy himself, Brock swayed against Chip Lang, face thrust close to the other's.

'If – *if* I see you around town after sundown, I'll kill you! You saw me shoot Cold-Deck so you know I can do it, and I will! Think you can remember that?'

Lang grinned bloodily through torn lips that had been mashed against his teeth. 'I'll remember *you!*'

He got out three filthy names before Brock's fist drove any more back down his throat. Lang's knees buckled but Brock held him against the tree by his forearm across the throat. Lang began to choke and gurgle, his eyes wide in panic now, arms flailing as he fought for breath.

'Brock! Don't *kill* him, man!' yelled Jake in alarm.

'Wouldn't dream of it. Just want to give him something to think about when he wakes *up!*'

And on this last word, Brock butted his head brutally

into Lang's face, feeling as well as hearing the nose squash to pulp.

Wiping blood from his own swollen, bruised face, swaying with fatigue, he let Lang fall in a ragged, bloody heap on the ground, as he heard a shocked voice say, 'My God! You – you're a merciless, callous *brute*, aren't you!'

It was Louisa Partridge.

Brock turned his head slowly and painfully on his bruised neck.

He looked at her coldly with his swelling, blackened eyes.

And he thought he saw her give a slight shiver. 'Why did you hire scum like that?'

'None of your damn business.'

'It is if you figure to send him after me an' Jake again. Likely cost you more, though, now he's taken a beating, he'll shake you down for every dollar he can.'

She seemed stunned. 'Is – is *that* what you think? I hired him to-to keep you away from me?' She made a derisive sound, almost like a genteel snort. 'You flatter yourself, mister! Chip was very close to my husband. They fought in the war together and Jim owed him his life! And he's been very helpful to me since Jim died.'

'Take my advice and get rid of him. The only one he's lookin' out for is Chip Lang – or whatever his real name is. He's a killer and a mighty mean one at that.'

Angrily, she snapped, 'Then perhaps *you*'d better watch out!'

His cold eyes went to her face. 'Somebody better.'

CHAPTER 11

OBLIGATIONS

He could sense the tension in her and her efforts to hide it. No, it's more than tension, he reckoned silently. It's fear. She's decided I'm a killer and now she doesn't know how to get herself out of this mess.

'I-I believe I suggested a little while back that we could get together and pool our knowledge and resources' she said suddenly, hesitantly.

'Seem to recall something like that. But it kinda flew out the window, didn't it? Got lost in name-calling or something.'

She flushed. Her small hands clenched into fists which she tried to hide by moving some of her clothing to cover them, then lifted one hand to run it through her hair.

'I've already said I'm sorry,' she snapped.

Inwardly, he smiled: she'd been backed into a corner and she didn't like it, *not one damn bit*!

But he felt no real animosity toward her; he had her down as someone who was simply out of her depth and wasn't sure how to find her way back.

'Lou, let's face it: this has all gotten outa hand. The gold we're after might not even be here. *No, no, wait*! It's grown into some kinda legend and legends have a habit of getting twisted and turned around by whoever's talkin' about 'em, as long as it makes a good yarn or guarantees a few more free drinks if it can be dragged out long enough.'

'I am not interested in free drinks!' she said tersely, and he saw immediately that she regretted making the irrelevant remark. He held up a hand, his face sober, waiting a few moments, letting her calm down.

'The gold's here or it isn't.'

'Oh! Who d'you think you're talking to? Some foolish schoolgirl?'

'I don't think you'd ever be mistaken for a schoolgirl, Lou— Wait up now! My God, you're touchy! What I'm trying to say is, why *don't* we do like you suggested a while back?' He waved a hand. 'Why *don't* we pool our resources and make a proper search? If we find the gold, we share it. If we don't find it. . . ?' He shrugged. 'We can try looking somewhere else or simply go home, convinced it's not here and mebbe never was here.'

His words sobered her: she still looked very tense, but there was a thoughtful frown on her rather pleasant face – and maybe a trace of alarm – but he thought she was giving his words some serious thought.

'But you – you *know* this place, don't you? I mean, you worked it while you were on prove-up. . . ?'

His smile was tight. 'Never had a chance to do much of that! Rode around it a couple of times, lookin' for places to make a start. But, Goddammit! I don't know it well enough to have a dozen or so places up my sleeve where the gold could be if it's not where the damn legend says. Places that I might check out after you've gone. Isn't that what's bothering you?'

She flushed, looked uncomfortable, but didn't speak.

'I'm getting kinda tired of your nasty remarks about my honesty. OK, we haven't found the gold and I'm rapidly getting to the point where I simply don't give a damn. Now, you want to try again, or you want to just quit and ride out? Right now, I don't care, either way.'

She was pale and maybe shaking a little at his genuinely angry tone. 'Look, I-I'm sorry I'm so suspicious. I didn't set out to insult you, though I can see now it *was* an insult and couldn't be mistaken for anything else but—'

'All right, all right!' he said roughly. 'How about we forget the whole damn thing? I'll make a fire and we can brew a cup of coffee and – well, who knows?'

She surprised him by smiling. 'I really am sorry for behaving like a greedy bitch.' She held out a small trembling hand. 'Can we go back to our original agreement to share anything of value we find? Will that be all right with you?'

After a long moment, his face rigid, he suddenly smiled crookedly and thrust out his hand.

'Shake, pardner.'

Jake looked from one to the other as they gripped

97

hands, jaw dropping slightly before he snapped it closed and shook his head solemnly.

'Lord help us,' he whispered to himself.

'You're bein' a bit hard on her, Brock,' Jake said, as he helped gather wood for the coffee fire. 'She's off-balance over not gettin' that insurance or whatever she was expectin' when her husband died. I reckon she's hard up and *needs* the money, that's why she's so' – he shrugged, looking a mite embarrassed – 'so testy. Don't want us to know she's hurting for cash.'

Brock looked at him steadily. 'You figure that out all by yourself?'

Jake flushed. 'Yeah, I did. I'm not an idiot, just because I'm young.'

'Never thought you were.' Brock spoke quietly, watching as Louisa took a coffee sack from her saddle-bags. 'Fact, I think you're right: she does need this gold.'

Jake blinked, surprised and pleased. 'Well, I guess if it *is* here we can share with her? I mean, seems fair don't it. . . ?'

Brock looked at him soberly, then smiled. He punched Jake lightly on the upper arm. 'Already gave my word on that.'

Jake grinned, let it fade slowly as Brock warned, 'But you stand with me, pardner, and that automatically makes you Lang's enemy . . . you ready for that?'

Jake nodded slowly, and spoke very softly, 'Already figured that.'

Brock Chase held Jake's gaze for a few seconds, then

smiled slightly. 'Guess I must've trained you pretty well after all.'

'But I wouldn't mind makin' sure *you*'re close by if ever Lang comes after me.'

'I'll be there, pard.'

'Hey! You men! You always talk about women gossiping!' called Louisa suddenly, holding up the coffee sack and some sourdough biscuits. 'How about getting that coffee brewing?'

'Gettin' right on with it, ma'am,' Jake called back, surprising Brock. 'Just bring the fixin's and we'll eat an' drink in about ten minutes.'

She nodded and by the time she had strolled across, the fire was lit and the pot of water rested on a couple of stones amidst the growing flames.

She seemed more sober than her tone had suggested when she'd needled them about getting the fire started.

'I think we need to get Chip to a doctor – or, rather, the doctor to him. I think he's hurt too badly to make the journey into town.'

Brock frowned. 'You think he's hurt that bad?'

'He's really seriously hurt, can hardly breathe,' she said abruptly, looking directly at Brock. 'In my opinion, he – well, he could even die.'

Brock chewed the mouthful of sourdough biscuit before answering. 'Then we *better* get a sawbones out here.'

Jake started. 'Brock! I-I know a sawbones is the best move but – Bronson and McBarr'll buy into it and you—'

Brock nodded slowly. 'Have to chance it, Jake. I

didn't set out to kill Lang.'

Louisa frowned slightly as she checked the coffee pot. 'If I was asked,' she said slowly. 'I think I'd have to give you an argument. I-I've already told you I thought all that brutality was unnecessary . . . without *any* pity.'

He nodded easily enough. 'Pity don't enter into it, Lou. It was a matter of who got the upper hand. If it'd been Lang, I reckon you'd be takin' me in now, draped over my saddle, either to the sawbones or, mebbe, the undertaker.'

She flushed and her lips compressed. 'I'll admit it was very brutal on both sides and Chip has had some terrible fights, but—'

'Bronson will love to see me in this kind of fix. Maybe you better ride in with Jake and I'll stay somewhere around here.'

'No, Brock!' Jake said loudly. 'You know Bronson'll put out a shoot-on-sight order for you! It's just what he's waiting for.'

'I won't allow that to happen,' Louisa said quickly. 'It was a dreadful fight, but it was – well, what I suppose you could call *fair* in its own brutal way.' There was defiance in the look she gave him. 'But I will see Chip gets proper medical attention; he's entitled to that.'

She paused and looked at him. He nodded solemnly. 'A fair enough view,' he admitted. 'For you, anyway.'

'I think so. It still makes me sick to my stomach, thinking about it, but I'll give Sheriff Bronson what I consider an honest, and unbiased opinion.'

Brock smiled crookedly. 'I believe you'll try your best, Lou, but it won't get you anywhere. Bronson'll have a dead-or-alive handbill circulatin' on me before the ink's dried. But you and Jake fetch the doctor for Lang. Tell 'em what happened; paint whatever kind of picture of me you feel like because it won't make any difference with Bronson: he won't pass up this chance to stretch my neck.'

Her hand was shaking as she lifted her biscuit towards her mouth, changed her mind and lowered the arm.

'I— Chip worked for me. Whether he was a good man or bad, I can't say for sure, but I do know he was helpful, very helpful, and considerate, when Jim was killed. Now he's badly hurt and needs medical attention. I really think it might be best if you head for the hills, as the saying goes, Brock Chase. Because I feel I'm *obligated* to give Chip whatever help he needs.'

'Yeah!' he said curtly. 'That part's clear enough. . . .' Then, abruptly, he got to his feet. 'I'd sure admire a cup of coffee, right now – maybe with a slug of whiskey in it, but I think I'd best be going. You can help Lou with Lang, can't you, Jake?'

'Sure. But, listen, Brock—'

Brock held up a hand. 'That's it. I'll get going. I know these hills tolerably well, so mebbe I can keep ahead of Bronson's posse. In any case, for now. . . .' He paused, threw a mock salute. '*Adios!*'

Her face was taut as she watched him check his six-gun as he walked away.

Jake took a step as if to follow him, but then stopped and, tight-lipped, watched the distance increase between them.

'Looks like you better stay here with Lang. I'll go fetch the doc,' he said.

'I was thinking the same thing, but—' Her tone hardened. 'I wouldn't want you to delay just so Brock has a better chance of getting away.'

Jake's young face was hard and he looked like he might even cuss. 'Think what you like. I'd rather stay with Brock, anyway. Why don't *you* fetch the law? That way you'll be sure Bronson'll get here in time to arrest him!'

Her mouth tightened but she nodded slowly. 'Perhaps that would be better. only I doubt there'll be any arrests. Why should there be?'

'You know well as I do Bronson hates Brock. And if he can manage to pin Lang's death on him, that's *if* he dies, of course. . . .'

She frowned, was silent for long seconds.

'I see! Well, I do know that Carl Bronson is a vindictive man. All right, I'll be moving along then. And I won't waste any time. You'd better not, either, if you know what I mean. . . ?'

Jake smiled slowly. 'Yes'm, I believe I do.'

CHAPTER 12

TRAPPED

Brock sat his mount on a tight, narrow trail behind a screen of thin brush. He leaned forward in the saddle, watching as Louisa left her spread: she must've decided to ride into town instead of Jake; she could probably better describe Lang's condition to the medico anyway.

She was putting the spurs to the mount's flanks and he felt a slight tightening of his belly muscles: Chip Lang must be in a bad way for her to hurry like that.

'His own damn fault,' Brock murmured to himself, although he wasn't proud of the fact that he had beaten any man so close to death. But Chip had been a true mean one and the only way to handle that sort was to be just as mean – or meaner – than they were.

The girl was a strange one, but tougher than she looked. He had no doubt she would describe the fight to the sheriff in all its gory details, but he figured she *would* be honest about it: both men had fought as if trying to kill each other, but whether or not Bronson would take this into account, or simply see Brock's efforts as just any means to victory.

'Well, reckon I can figure out the answer to that one, knowing how Bronson's brain works.'

He watched Louisa ride out of sight, turned back in time to see Jake going back into the house – pausing slightly and looking around casually – hand close to gun butt.

Brock straightened slowly in the saddle and looked around at the jumble of hills – some brush-and-tree-clad, some looked almost naked, with short grass covering them. All of them were possible hideouts which he knew he was going to need – and soon.

'Mebbe the further away the better,' he mused, and was starting to lift his horse's reins to make his move, but stopped abruptly, the animal snorting a protest at the apparent sudden change of his rider's mind.

'*No!*' Brock said quietly. 'Bronson'll expect me to go deep into the hills – so, I'll take a chance and stick close to the ranch. That way, I can see what's going on, too.'

Decision made, he looked up at the hill behind him. It would give him a good overall view of the ranch, but the way up didn't offer much in the way of cover.

Still, it would be a while yet before Bronson and McBarr came with their posse. He would have time to find himself a safe position that would allow him to see what was going on.

He hoped!

Louisa Partridge was surprised at the speed with which

Sheriff Carl Bronson organized a posse once she had told him, after first seeing the sawbones, about Chip Lang's injuries.

'Lang'll be no loss if he does kick it,' growled McBarr, reaching for his hat on a wall peg in Bronson's office.

'He kicks it, Chase goes up for murder,' answered the sheriff and Louisa said swiftly, 'Hardly that, Sheriff! It was a-a terribly savage brawl, but I have to be honest and say it was on both sides. The men were equally brutal with one another.'

Bronson looked up as he reached for his hat off the peg next to his chair. He started to rise as he was jamming the hat on his balding head.

'When you're scared of bein' beat to death, you fight back with whatever you can: kick, bite, scratch—'

'And head-butt?' Louisa cut in swiftly, and watched his mouth tighten and his eyes narrow.

'Depends, don't it? If Chase was the main aggressor and he head-butted Chip—' He shrugged. 'That'd count as a – how'd you call it, Brady? An aggressive blow? A—'

'I'd call it a damn *murderous* blow, Sheriff,' McBarr said coldly. 'A head-butt can be mighty dangerous.'

Louisa started to protest, but Bronson was checking the loads in his six gun by now, and nodded almost absently.

'Yeah, I agree.' He flicked his hard gaze to the girl's now alarmed face. 'Your friend Chase is in a lot of trouble, Miz Partridge. We'll just take a small posse, Brady, he can't get far in them hills if he don't know 'em.'

'Brock?' she demanded. 'It wasn't a *deliberate* thing. It was a *fight*! All kinds of blows are delivered when two men are fighting. You already admitted that, and with not much thought given to the damage they may do.'

'An' if one's so badly injured he dies—' Bronson shook his head briefly. 'Well, the other is in a lot of trouble. That's the law, ma'am. Brady, get half-a-dozen men who know them hills, just in case he's— Er, where you goin', Miz Partridge—?'

Making for the door of the cramped office, Louisa was startled to see how fast Brady McBarr had moved: he now stood between her and the exit, smirking.

'I have other business to do while I'm in town—'

'Well, now, I appreciate you've rid a long ways and you might's well do any shoppin' while you're here, ma'am, but I'll need a written statement from you. Brady, call Deputy Daniels in, will you? He can stay with Miz Partridge while she writes her statement.' He smiled – on-off – without humour. 'You'll be free to do your shoppin' then, Miz Partridge. You did the right thing, comin' in and tellin' me of the troubles you're havin' with this damned hardcase—'

'I'm not having any trouble with him! We're just trying to do what's right and fetch the doctor for Chip Lang and to advise you of the situation.'

The sheriff held up a hand, face unsmiling. 'What you still standin' there for, Brady? Organize that posse now, or we'll get to the damn ranch an' find Chase has vamoosed!'

Louisa's legs felt suddenly weak and she sat down heavily in the hard office chair as McBarr left in a hurry.

'Sheriff, this isn't necessary. It—'

'Don't you fret, Miz Partridge. We'll do things smoothly as possible, an' by the book. Now, you start your statement – paper an' pen in front of you – and I'll get Mrs Bronson to bring you a cup of coffee. That meet with your approval?'

'I suppose it has to,' she said tightly and Bronson's lips moved slightly.

It may have been meant for a smile. 'Ah! Here's Deputy Daniels at last. Make yourself comfortable, ma'am. Shouldn't take long to bring in Chase . . . before he tries to kill someone else.'

Louisa looked startled as she put a hand to her mouth, eyes wide in alarm.

'*No, no! You have it all wrong!*'

'Just write that statement, ma'am. We'll sort out the legal angles all right. Daniels! Give Miz Partridge that pen so she can get started . . . and stay with her till we get back.'

She looked up sharply as the sheriff started to move towards the door. 'Where – where're you going, Sheriff?'

'Thought it was obvious, Miz Partridge. We're gonna see what Doc says about Lang's condition, then we may – or may not – have to arrest Brock Chase. It could be a murder charge, so we're goin' armed.'

Down below the cliff, where he was sitting on a rock rolling a cigarette, Brock heard the horse carefully picking its way through the almost invisible narrow crack in the rock-studded walls.

It was Jake who had shown him the place, but as a warning, telling him, 'Good hideout country up here, Brock, but don't try to quit it by that crevice unless you really have to.' The young cowpoke had shown him the zigzag crack in the walls.

'Looks like you could lead a hoss through there,' Brock had allowed. 'Be tight and might scare him some, but I figure an average bronc could make it.'

'If he liked the rider – who wouldn't be in the saddle – just no room for that. But mebbe if a man had a hoss's trust he could use it, but *not* if he was in a hurry. He'd only bust a knee cap, or, worse, get the hoss stuck.'

Brock was examining the passage as Jake spoke. 'Be tight all right – a desperate man might make it, though.'

'He'd have to be desperate.'

'Where's it come out?'

'I found it when we were on our prove-up spreads. I was after a wild dog that'd been botherin' a couple of my young steers. I spotted him and took a shot at him, without thinkin'—'

'What? You fired a gun in a narrow slot like that? With all them twists an' turns, and—? You're lucky it didn't ricochet and kill you!'

Jake was actually blushing. 'I was mad at the damn dog! Think my hands were shakin' for a week after I realized what a fool thing I did.'

'Yeah, well? Where does it come out?'

'Never got right through, but I *think* it's one of them.' He pointed to the sandstone face of the cliff above where there were three twisted cracks showing

108

under an overhang.

'Hell, from here, I doubt you'd ever get a horse in or out of any of those.'

'N-no, but it gives you one helluva good view of all them canyons below it that sweep on to the plains. I-I climbed one of the walls one time just to see – in case it might come in handy some time.'

Brock shook his head slowly, then smiled. 'You're teachin' *me* now, pard` And doing a good job. If they come lookin' for me, I'll mebbe use one of them cracks to see which canyon they camp in, and so on.'

'You're bigger'n me, so you'll have to watch you don't get stuck. Likely be the beer-belly that does it.'

Jake grinned and tried to jump out of reach, but Brock was too fast, caught his wrist and pulled him back hard. 'Well, I tell you, if *you* ever get stuck and I come along, I'll get you free all right, with a damn good kick in the seat of your pants, like – *this*!'

'*Nononono! Don't do it! Geez, Brock – don't!*'

Brock was surprised at the sound of real panic in the other's voice and the way he was struggling and trying to push Brock into the crack.

'Take it easy! Hell, I'm only joshin'.'

'Goddamnit! Look there! Will you *look*!'

Jake was pointing even as he used his lean body to try to force Brock at least part-way into the narrow crack.

'In the middle canyon! See 'em? Seven riders, and the sun's winkin' off badges on their shirts. That's a posse comin', Brock, an' headin' right this way.'

Alert now, Brock watched the riders down below and, even as he did so, he saw two of them point and wave

109

madly to catch the attention of Sheriff Bronson, in the lead.

'Hell! We been spotted!' Brock said, following the words with a curse. 'Be too damn slow to try to force our way back through the cleft now . . . they'd pick us off while havin' a cup of coffee.'

'Yeah,' Jake said heavily. 'I think we're trapped! We're gonna have to learn how to dodge lead, Brock!'

'*And in a damned hurry!*'

CHAPTER 13

WALL-TO-WALL

They made easy targets up there, silhouetted against the paleness of the shale wall.

The ledge they were on was narrow and broken-edged. They couldn't turn around in a hurry – too risky: they could easily overbalance and topple down into the canyon.

'Must've got a posse together pretty damn quick,' panted Jake, shuffling along and ducking as lead struck only a foot above his head, showering him with shale. 'Hell! They ain't foolin'! *Hey! What the*—?'

'In!' gritted Brock, his hand pushing against Jake's shoulders. 'You had the right idea before: *get in here*!'

Jake resisted. 'You loco? I just been tellin' you, showin' you what can happen in that narrow space—!'

'I know, we both *know*! So do they! Now get in that crevice as far as you can. I'll be right behind you.'

Jake blinked but then Brock's hands roughly pushed

111

and forced him past the first curved lip.

'Hell almighty!' he gritted. 'We'll be picked off like fish in a barrel with all them ricochets!'

'Move, dammit!'

Brock pushed and twisted, bones creaking, grunting and cursing under his breath as he wormed in after the reluctant Jake. 'We're s-stuck, damn you, Brock!'

'Kneel!'

'How the hell can I—?'

'Stretch your legs, one behind the other, like you're running, then drop to your knees!'

'You're crazy! I – aw, shoot! What'd you hit me for? Oh. Listen, Brock—' Then Jake suddenly stopped complaining. 'What the—?'

'Just noticed it, huh? Them rock bulges? None of 'em is any lower than knee-height – there's space underneath to stretch out flat, and by hell, we better get it done pronto!'

He said this last in a rush of words as bullets screamed and buzzed at a man's head-height as the posse fired their rifles into the crack, urged on by Brady McBarr, the man's voice unmistakable even through the rattle of rifle fire.

'Hell's teeth!' groaned Jake. 'We – we can't be lucky all the time! We're gonna get hit sooner or later.'

'Make it later! Now get down on your belly and stretch out on the ground. Hug it like it's the best-looking dance-hall gal you've ever seen!'

'You're crazy! We'll—'

'That oughta hold 'em!' a voice drifted in from outside, up on the ridges. 'Not even a snake could live through that.'

'Well . . .' another voice answered cautiously, 'I-I'm goin' easy, just in case.'

They could hear the possemen arguing half-heartedly as they made their way out from the ridges.

'They're almost here,' Jake rasped.

'Well, move. Come on! They won't see us. You can tell by the voices they're way down in the trench at the bottom of the ridge which means we're above 'em. Move! Now, dammit, Jake! Now!' He heard Jake swear and asked, 'Where does it come out?'

'Dunno for sure. Somewhere near where the ridges stop—'

'OK. That means they'll still be looking for our bodies back here. How far to the Partridge place? No, wait! Looks like sundown, or close to it by the colour of the bit of sky I can see now. We're in luck: we're gonna be able to travel in the dark.'

'To Lou Partridge's place? Man, Bronson'll be watchin' an' waitin'!'

'And while he is, we'll slip across to my place again and get us some fresh mounts.'

'You really did check out this neck of the woods before signin'-on for prove-up, didn't you?'

'Always like to know there's a back door handy.'

After a short silence, Jake said quietly, 'I sure as hell would like to know what you're on the dodge for.'

'Mebbe I'll tell you someday.'

'Aw, *that day*! Think I know it – it's the day the birds start flyin' backwards to keep the dust outa their eyes, ain't it?'

'That's the one.'

Jake murmured some unintelligible reply and, afterwards, he thought maybe it was just as well it was unintelligible ... or Brock might rattle his teeth for him.

The possemen were divided: some wanted to go in through the crevice where Brock and Jake had entered, the others favoured the exit end where the posse would be gathering now.

'Listen to 'em,' Brock said in a low voice. 'Gettin' so hot under the collar I figure they might start shootin' at each other any damn time.'

'Yeah, they sure are arguin' But you notice one thing. . . ?'

'What've I missed?'

'They're all certain-sure we're dead.'

'That's good. A leetle bit or over-confidence in the hunters is one of the best things a fugitive can hope for, Jake. And we're not only on the run, we're under a shoot-on-sight order. We need to use the time while they're arguin', or we're gonna be dodgin' a dozen itchy trigger-fingers. C'mon, let's go.'

Sundown favoured them.

It sank quickly, without any lingering blaze of wild colour, and it sank behind the hill with the cliff face, so dropping a night-dark shadow over the very country that the pair wanted to cross.

If they exercised a little caution and kept their mounts quiet, it was just possible they might make it.

'We'll be able to get around the base of the cliff – too

114

dark to silhouette us now. Then make our way to the horses.'

Jake's voice rose in his excitement and he stiffened when Brock told him sharply to '*Shut the hell up!*'

'Listen, I ain't about to take that kinda talk from you or anyone else—!'

'You will, or I'll bend my Colt's barrel over your head. Just go quietly and we'll be back in our saddles again before you know it.'

They made it. Neither fully believing it.

The posse was stumbling about in the dark, sure they had killed both fugitives in the crevice tunnel, not worrying about making a noise now. Their rowdy over-confidence even helped to cover the stealthy movements of Jake and Brock as they moved through the dark, hoping their mounts wouldn't whinny in a greeting of recognition.

Brock just managed to clamp a hand across the lips of his horse as it shook its head and began a welcome snort.

'Yeah, yeah. Glad to see you, too, old pard,' he said in a low voice, stroking its neck, and felt it relax some. 'Come on now, let me lead. Jake? You OK with your mount?'

'Sure, he ain't pampered like your crowbait.'

'We just have a good relationship. Now let's move, we're crowdin' our luck.'

Jake's 'no answer' was answer enough and he fell in behind the dim shadow of Brock Chase and his mount.

They didn't move in total silence: it couldn't be helped when the mounts kicked two stones together, or

115

slid a couple of feet on a patch of gravel. Each time they stopped dead in their tracks, straining to hear over the heavy breathing of the horses.

'How close are we to that posse?' Brock asked, annoyed that he couldn't make out any landmarks he was able to identify.

'Ought to be right above 'em. *Yeah*! Straight down. They've brewed coffee and some of the ashes are still glowin'. Man, Brady McBarr'll skin 'em alive if he sees that.'

'Long as it's them he skins an' not us.'

Brock grunted louder than he meant to as he suddenly stepped off a raised section and stumbled as he fought for balance and a fast-groping hold on a protruding stone – that pulled right out of the cliff-face, spilling dirt and stones.

Below, one of the posse yelled. '*Hey!* I heard somethin'! Right above us. Could they be—?'

'They must be jammin' rags in their ears to shut out the damn noise you're makin'!' snapped Brady McBarr, hoarsely. 'I'll have you talkin' soprano you don't shut the hell up!'

Damn fool's making more noise than the other man, thought Brock. Both he and Jake had frozen, like a pair of sculptures, instinctively pressing as close as they could to the cliff-face.

There was a short, profane argument below and then the posse made enough noise to be mistaken for a cavalry troop preparing to charge into battle. Almost frantically, Deputy McBarr urged them to keep on with the search.

Then someone started shooting.

Two gunflashes down below, the snarl of a ricocheting bullet from the cliff-face and both fugitives literally clung by their nails as they tried to keep their mounts quiet – and with as firm a footing on the narrow trail as possible.

McBarr was screaming curses and the man he directed them at shouted back angrily that he was damned if he was going to be insulted by some jumped-up deputy and—

'*Goddamnit to hell!*' McBarr yelled in frustration, throwing caution to the winds now in his anger. 'They'll be ten goddamn miles away by now with all this racket! *Judas priest! Shut up, the lot of you.* We'll never catch 'em, thanks to you damn fools!'

More profanity. Then even more! And a full-blown argument got underway, half-a-dozen voices raised while Brock and Jake, grinning tightly, made their way slowly across the black cliff face and started down a precarious trail to the bottom, well past the scene of the posse's squabble.

'Townsmen!' Brock said quietly, helping Jake around a jutting boulder. 'Make the worst kinda posse once you get 'em away from home-cookin' and cuddlin' the missus.'

Jake didn't answer for a few seconds, then said quietly, 'You sound like you're talkin' from experience?'

'Time to hush up, kid! We're passin' close to those idiots now.'

Jake smiled tightly. 'Well, I'll be damned,' he said in

a barely audible whisper. 'Reckon I might have a rene-gade lawman for a pard.'

The posse was breaking up, men arguing so intently they were no longer worrying about – perhaps only barely aware of – what they were supposed to be doing there.

Until, in a brief hiatus while the arguing townsmen were catching their breaths, someone held up a hand and said sharply, 'Listen! Listen, you goddamn fools!' The desperation in the voice made them pause and— 'Hell, there they go!'

They all heard it then: the fading sounds of gallop-ing horses.

CHAPTER 14

CAPTURE

I think Brock's right, Jake told himself as they both galloped through the night. Townsmen do make lousy possemen once they're away from all their home comforts.

Brock was slightly ahead on his big black. Jake knew the horse was faster and had more stamina than the roan he forked. He had agreed that they should keep a distance between them – being practical, it made sense. Nothing to be gained by both of them being captured . . . nor even one, for that matter.

He was suddenly aware that Brock had dropped back and was holding the big black in right alongside of him.

'There's a turn into a canyon somewhere ahead,' Brock said, his words fighting against the wind of his horse's passage. 'You take it, I'll make for the hills.'

'They got some fast mounts,' Jake reminded him. 'Once they hit the wide-open spaces they'll tear up the night to reach the hills an' they got plenty of men to do it.'

'That's why we separate. My hoss can climb the hills better and faster than yours. You lead 'em away from me. You shouldn't have any trouble across the flats – long as you know somewhere you can hide out. . . ?'

'I know. But I don't like the idea of you bein' trapped in them hills.'

'Me neither, so I'll make sure I don't *get* trapped. I know 'em tolerably well by now. But what about you on the flats?'

'Can find my way around 'em pretty good. Listen, you know that place they call Busted Gut? Where the river burst it banks last rainy season, cut clear through a big section of O'Hara's land and flooded them farms near—'

'I know it, sort of,' Brock cut in.

'It's near the spot where they put up a marker to show where there'd been a big battle at the end of the war. Three hundred Rebs were surrounded an'—'

'Been there,' Brock said, in clipped tones. 'I was one of the three hundred. Started executin' us in batches of two or three dozen. Lucky the Armistice was signed before they got to my bunch.'

'Yeah, rotten times, all right? Well, *behind* The Gut, as they call it, you'll find—'

'The Skillet – right?'

'How you know about that?'

'I managed to slip into a wagon one night and they went there – a dead-straight trail in, and a near-perfect circle of big boulders: like a skillet with its handle. I've looked it over, but if you're thinking of using it, well, I dunno, Jake. It's easy enough to get into, but gettin' out. . . .' He looked and sounded mighty dubious.

'Oh, sure, lotsa folk know about it, but most stay away because of the rattlers.'

'Rattlers. Snakes, in a nice place like that?'

'Yeah, by the dozen, mebbe the hundreds.'

'Hell, that's a damn pity.'

'One of them nasty tricks of nature. But, if you don't wet your pants every time you hear a rustle, there's a good place to hide by a sorta natural arch just up from the lake.'

'Ye-ah, I think I saw that arch – almost hid by giant boulders but slightly sticks up above 'em?'

'That's it. How about we meet there? Say, give each other – aw, two, no longer'n three days to get there? If one of us don't show up in that time—'

Brock looked at him closely. 'I'll wait a day extra.'

'Brock, you can't risk it. We've got a small lead now but we gotta make use of it.'

Which, of course, made good sense and Brock nodded slowly.

'We better move, whatever else we do. They'll be searching down this way soon as it gets light enough.' he thrust out his hand and they shook briefly. 'If I get caught, don't try to rescue me. No sense in us both—'

'Yeah, I agree,' Jake broke in. 'See you somewhere, huh?'

'*Hasta la vista*, kid!'

They went their separate ways and Brock, sober now, knew damn well if he was captured, this young ranny

121

would bust a gut trying to break him free no matter what!

Of course, he'd do the same for Jake, but, well, that was different.

He was older, had more experience at busting out of prisons.

Jake was the unlucky one.

He rode well, found and kept to reasonable cover, but the sky was lightening by the minute and his roan went lame on him.

It was just past the entrance to The Skillet. He had deliberately passed it by, knowing there was a place not far ahead, screened by rocks and a bunch of trees that had suffered during the last big storm – criss-crossed trunks and big rocks that had fallen from the edge of the low cliff above made a good screen from anyone down on the flats. Maybe he had forgotten that the men who were on his trail were *locals*, knew this country as well as they knew their own names. Whatever, Jake grew just a mite over-confident and put his mount up a slope with lots of small stones scattered about underfoot. It would be no trouble for a fresh mount, dodging the double-fist-sized hazards, but his horse was tired, had had rough treatment – necessary at the time – in rough country, as Jake tried to dodge the posse.

The first stumble warned him but, looking back over his left shoulder, he saw part of the posse burst out of a screen of brush and the lead rider pointed immediately in his direction. The weary mount was just a mite too tired to make it to cover soon enough.

Two shots were triggered skyward by the man and the posse immediately closed up their ranks and—

Jake had looked back for too long.

Half-hipped in the saddle he had let one rein hang loose and the horse mistook it as its rider's signal to veer the opposite way. It did: and crashed through a thicket that edged the gully he hadn't seen.

It was a toss-up who made the most noise: the horse with its shrill protest as the crumbling edge of the gully gave way underfoot, or Jake, as he felt himself involuntarily lifting out of the saddle. Too late to yank the reins back the other way. *Damnit!* He tried, of course, but—

He instinctively threw an arm across his face as thorny branches raked his front, tearing his shirt, and chest and the left side of his face.

He yelled again, but this time it was drowned by the roan's whickering and then he was somersaulting, bushes parting with his passage until he stopped abruptly as he struck the ground and a fireworks display exploded inside his skull.

Even through its roaring and the crashing of the fall he heard the horses behind and above coming up and, just before oblivion claimed him, a harsh, victorious voice bawled, 'Got the bastard! Right where we want him!'

Brock Chase heard those words, too.

Fainter, of course, as he was on the other side of the gully, hidden by deep brush, patting his panting mount's neck, making low, soothing sounds and trying to stop it stamping its feet. His gun was in his hand, but

123

although he had cocked the hammer, he lowered it again almost immediately.

Eight or ten men – armed men, and out for blood.

Pointless to try and rescue Jake at this stage, so he backed up the sweating black, took one last look in time to see three men grab the semi-conscious Jake and struggle with him as they held his wrists and clamped them painfully into handcuffs.

The kid took half-a-dozen blows to the body and one back-hander across the face from none other than Deputy Brady McBarr himself. Brock tightened his grip on the gun butt as he saw Jake's legs buckle and his head snap back with the force of the blow, blood smearing across his cheek.

But there was nothing he could do that would gain either of them a chance at freedom.

Not right now.

It wasn't long though before he decided he should do something.

They beat-up Jake. McBarr had him held and pummelled him with a series of rapid blows to the body, kicked the kid's legs out from under him and, when he fell on to his side, walked around him, boots thudding into the lean young body.

'Where's that sonofabitch Chase? Huh? Where, damn you!'

Brock gritted his teeth so hard he thought they might break. His hand must have left its imprint in the butt of his gun as he watched. He didn't know how much longer he would be able to hold himself back.

But it would be suicide for him to try to rescue Jake now with all those guns waiting 'though he guessed that this was the intent of Brady McBarr: beat-up on Jake mighty hard until Brock would just have to try to rescue him no matter what the risk and, of course, would be shot down in the attempt.

'Sorry, Jake,' he said half-aloud. 'All that'd happen is that I'd be shot down or captured, too. Do neither of us and good.'

He hoped Jake could hold out.

The whole damned day stretched ahead of them now. Posse and fugitives.

But as soon as it was dark enough, Brock would somehow slip in past any guards they had on Jake and – well, *then* they would see! He dearly hoped that McBarr would take a turn at guarding Jake.

But Brady McBarr had other plans.

Instead of handcuffing Jake to a tree or a suitable rock, the posse mounted up and Jake, at the end of a rope, hands still in the constricting cuffs, was set afoot behind the deputy's mount, and they made their way back towards town.

Brock's belly tightened. He almost cut loose with a string of curses as Jake fell and was dragged, until McBarr slowed enough for him to get groggily to his feet.

Then they started riding again, Jake half the time being dragged, the other half trying to run fast enough to stay – almost – on his feet.

That damned McBarr. There was no doubt he aimed to lock Jake up in the town jail.

Then wait and see what Brock would do about *that*!

The brutal deputy even stood over the semi-conscious Jake once, cupped his hands around his mouth and called, 'We'll be waitin', Chase. Me an' Jake! It's gonna be a l-o-n-g night.' A pause, then, 'We ain't had a breakout from our jail in ten years! That tell you anythin'?'

CHAPTER 15

NO GOOD NEWS

Brock didn't see any sign of them at first, but he knew blamed well that McBarr would leave at least some men hidden while he rode openly toward town with Jake as his prisoner.

So he hung back near The Skillet area, did a little quiet scouting, and finally found there were three – at least – holed-up in that wild country.

One fool was even smoking – and a pipe at that, the pungent odour of the tobacco drifting in the hot air.

He made a note of where the man was, the cloud of smoke marking it like a sign-post. The other two were harder to locate but, being townsmen and used to company, drifted together in a creekbed where they watered their horses and sat on a rock chatting.

But they looked around often, one man climbing a

ridge with his rifle, checking for signs of Brock. Not finding any, he climbed back down to join his companion, who turned out to be none other than the big, brutal man with the heavy black frontier moustache.

He was hunkered down beside a rock above a narrow trail that led to a small, platform-like ledge that would give a good view over the area.

'Lookin' for someone else to soften up before you turn 'em over to McBarr?' Brock asked quietly and the man, squatting in the shade, started so violently, he fell over, dropped his rifle, but lunged wildly after it.

He grunted when Brock's boot pinned his right hand to the rocky ground, and yelled when Brock's gun barrel knocked his hat off as it clipped him above the right ear. He fell backwards, half-sitting, blinking, the ear bleeding a little, but he made no sound now as he stared down the steady barrel of Brock's menacing gun.

He lifted a pair of wary eyes.

Brock nudged him in the side, made him turn face down. The man grunted as his gun was kicked out of reach. 'Now, roll over on your back.'

The man obeyed, one hand rising to half-cover his face. 'Listen, I-I'm just a townsman! Din' have no choice but to ride along. You don't argue with McBarr, or Bronson.'

'Or me,' Brock told him quietly and the man tensed. 'Now, see if you can tell me the truth when I ask you a few questions.'

The man jerked his head back as Brock made a feint with the gun, the barrel just missing his nose above that black moustache.

128

'But first, move your butt – more, dammit! All right. Now, stay put.' The man squirmed and Brock frowned. 'Wait up! What's this?'

Brock stooped quickly and picked up the ring of keys that had half-fallen from the other's hip pocket. He shook them in front of the man's angry face.

'That solves one problem.' Brock rattled the keys again. 'These for the cells down below?' The man simply stared, but when Brock drew back his right foot, nodded vigorously. 'Good. Now just keep it up and tell me about the jailhouse.'

The man blinked. 'Hell, I dunno nothin' about no damn jail!'

'Don't *lie*! You tellin' me you never been locked up for gettin' drunk on a Saturday night?'

'Aw, well, yeah . . . but—'

Brock's gun muzzle rammed into the man's right ear and he yelped. 'Tell me the layout, or I'll fire this gun right alongide your ear so you never hear again.'

'Jesus, man! Don't play so damn rough!'

'Who's playin'? I'm asking you for help. Might be to your advantage to give me some. Want to think it over?'

The man looked sly now: just for an instant, but Brock could see he was thinking he had an advantage here. Which he did, but Brock didn't aim to let him get used to the idea.

So he tapped him on the nose with the gunbarrel hard enough for the nostrils to ooze a little blood. He yelped again, fell on his side. His eyes were wide and full of fear now . . . more so than earlier as he watched Brock slip his hunting knife from his belt sheath. The man froze as the blade rested under his nose on that moustache 'Hey, easy! What you doin'?'

'Just wonderin' what you look like without all that bush under your nose.' The man squirmed, eye bulging, shaking his head. 'No? Well, answer my questions, and if I even *think* you're lyin'. . . .'

He pressed with the knife blade again and the man cringed under his quickly raised arm. 'I-I dunno much, but I'm tellin' you – gospel – you'll never get the kid outa there. Tougher men than you've tried bustin' someone out.'

'Well, I'll decide *after* you tell me the layout – *if you ever get started*!' Brock raised his gun.

'*Wait*, wait! I-I'll tell you what I can!'

'You're a lot smarter than you look, friend. Let's hear what you have to say . . . *now*!'

'I dunno much. Sheriff just uses me for – well, you know.'

'Yeah, the bully-boy. Soften up someone already scared white. Well, mister, I'm all ears.'

The townsman cleared his throat and began to talk.

When he had finished, Brock knew that, even with the keys to the cells below, it was not going to be an easy job to break Jake out and get away.

Originally, it had been a barracks for the cavalry troop that had been stationed in this area during the latter part of the War.

Heavy log walls still stood and could withstand a hail of bullets, and likely a barrage of some of the lighter cannon balls. But it was built on a steep slope which had been dug away beneath and bricked in. Some of the foundations were actual boulders, set solidly and deep in the soil of the slope, partially supporting sections of brickwork, to make the lower block of cells.

But there was no ground-level access: the lower storey had to be entered from the floor above, which meant first going up into the timbered part of the jail, and even there heavily armed guards stood by.

Naturally, the most important inmates – or the toughest – were kept in the lower section. There were only a few windows cut into the stone walls, each heavily barred with iron rods.

It was a hangover from the War. The Union had set up a veritable operations centre here when they had made an all-out attack in the hope of ending the fighting, only to be met by unexpected resistance, so strong that they were driven back, abandoning all papers and maps and even stashes of weapons in their sudden retreat. A victory for the South that was never repeated, but would be long remembered in the history books.

Brock knew all this, having actually taken part in one of the raids that had left this place manned only by a skeleton crew until it was finally abandoned. But as remembered hatred had dwindled over the passing years the place was all but forgotten. Then, when the post-War outlaws became a real problem, it was reopened as a military post, the lower section refurbished into iron-barred cells that would need dynamite to open them if ever the keys were lost. Naturally, it was a foregone conclusion that here was where Sheriff Bronson would put Jake Cash.

And he did, confident that the young renegade could not escape or be rescued. Trouble was, he didn't know Brock Chase as well as he thought he did. For a start, 'Brock Chase' wasn't his real name. Not that it mattered, but it was Vance McCall from San Angelo, Colorado.

He had fought for the South during the War, naturally, and when the cause was obviously lost, made for Mexico with hundreds of other Rebs who had some crazy idea of forming an avenging army south of the border.

Of course, it never happened, and on one of the many raids on the group, Vance was captured and thrown into a prison specially built for rebel prisoners – stone walls and natural rock base: 'Escape-proof' was confidently marked on most maps, but— *Not quite.*

At least three men escaped from the hellhole that was mockingly termed HSH – short for Home Sweet Home – Vance McCall wasn't one of them, but his brother, Homer, was.

Dying in Vance's arms after he had been recaptured and tortured by way of punishment, Homer had never divulged his secret as the last man to escape HSH.

Except, his last gasping words to Vance had been: '*P-puerta – tres – r-roca*'.

The third rock is the door.

Brock had never known just what Homer meant but he remembered the words simply because they *had* been the last ones ever spoken by his brother.

And now he had seen the prison – these days simply called the Jailhouse, an upper timber cell-section,

132

above a base of natural boulders holding *more* cells –
those words began to make some sort of sense.

    If only a man knew where to start counting.

CHAPTER 16

HOW TO MOVE A MOUNTAIN

The theory was that even if a prisoner did somehow manage to get out of his cell, he had nowhere to go.

Down in the stone-walled section it was near freezing, little or no sun reaching the area. Lanterns were few and far between – turned low in any case – so that it seemed like perpetual night, at best only half-light, to the prisoners.

They squinted, full daylight hurting their eyes, and this was also seen as a good deterrent as it would certainly slow down any escape attempt.

After all the trouble it would take for the cell door to be somehow breached in the first place, anything else that slowed down the escape would be one more obstacle – and even close to nerve-shattering for any man in that position, strung out like a bow, taut and quivering.

And, always supposing he *did* make it to the stairs leading to the floor above which was highly unlikely, they twisted in a deliberate steep climb, the treads at different heights and widths making it a real hazard that had been the literal downfall of many a futile escape attempt.

That, of course, was a theoretical attempt from the inside, but, if somehow, the prisoner intent on escape had outside help. . . .

We-ell, firstly, how could there be?

It would mean someone had to come in through the upstairs cell block, which had guards and locked doors and even some booby traps on darkened stairways, already hazardous for the incautious. Which was why the few prison maps that existed were still marked with the familiar 'Escape-proof'.

But, reasoned Brock Chase, what if there was no top section to worry about?

'That would sure make it easier,' he said aloud. 'but how could that be managed?'

It would take a battery of cannon, a dozen cases of dynamite . . . and likely kill everyone, prisoner or any lawman, upstairs or down.

'You need a better plan than that, *amigo*,' he told himself reluctantly. 'A much better plan.'

He was surprised how quickly the answer came to him.

'Fire! Holy Hell! The jail's on *fire*!'

He cupped a hand over his mouth to disguise his voice, although he figured no one would be worrying about who was raising the alarm, only the alarm itself.

And there was plenty of visual evidence of that!

The long timber section of the prison, sitting atop the brick and boulder base, was a mass of flames: they were all around the wooden walls above the more substantial lower cell-block.

But it looked like everything was burning, the flames crackling, smoke swirling: there was no glass in the windows only iron bars, four or five vertical ones in narrow windows, a few laced in a square pattern for the more elongated horizontal types.

His wild, urgent calls were unnecessary: with the prison on a rise, it was able to be seen from all over town as the flames increased.

The population surged in to watch and some to help get the upstairs prisoners out and under guard, others trying to fight the fire: but it had too good a hold for them to make much progress.

Everyone was concerned about the prisoners below – those they knew about, of course – and half the world must have heard their yells and panicky screams, Brock figured. He admitted he was a mite worried: he hadn't thought it would take hold so quickly or with such fury.

Fire and flames rose naturally, but blazing timbers broke loose and dropped, some resting against the few narrow window-spaces of the under-section, still burning.

But there were only three or four prisoners in the lower cell block – Jake and two others as it turned out – each with a cramped cell to himself.

Even their combined voices calling for help were

almost drowned out by the racket raised by those trying to fight the blaze above, and the destruction it was causing.

Crouched in the shadows, although they were lit intermittently by the sudden flare of flames, Brock had to wait his chance and hope Jake would survive – and the other two prisoners whoever they were.

His main problem was trying to find the boulder that Homer had named as being the way out – or in – the *puerta*.

'*The third rock. . . .*'

Brock stared for the hundredth time at the handful of boulders that acted as a natural base for the bricked-up cell block.

'Eight of the sonuvers,' he murmured. 'Now which way do I start counting to find the third one. . . ?'

A blast of heated air swept over him and he ducked, held an arm across his scorched face, seeing townsmen also ducking and running for cover. Coughing, he stumbled to his knees and some unknown samaritan helped him up and leaned him back against the hot wall – just for a second – then he leapt instinctively to the left. It was an unconscious movement, his survival instincts taking over.

But he found himself in between two boulders, which meant a gap that hadn't been noticeable before, a gap that – that would break the line.

He stepped back, eyes watering, but seeing the others on this side were making their way around to the front.

'Christ!' he breathed. Here he was in a break in the

137

line of boulders. All he had to do was count to the third one. But which way? Three to the right? Or three to the left?

'Hurry it up,' he told himself and knew he had to do something *pronto*. Or it would be all for nothing.

He stopped there and made his decision.

'Left!' No particular reason, just that the third rock on that side had a sort of sunken oval in it, part of the rock itself, but below the main bulge, and—

He tore the skin off his hands and knuckles and in seconds knew it was no use. He spun towards another boulder, counting from the one beside him and, as he reached for the third rock, he suddenly dropped his hands, spun back towards that one with the oval depression.

He had felt the rock *move* – only slightly, no more than a slight tilting, as if it was lightly balanced on something uneven that allowed it to tip or turn an inch or two. God! Was that all. . . ? 'Just a leetle bit more,' he whispered. 'Come on!'

It tilted. No secret panels. Just the way it was balanced on whatever supported it. He even heard the grinding of the base and then there was a choking blast of thick air and he glimpsed a dark gap between the rock and the wall. Barely enough for a man to squeeze through, but—

He was already sucking in his chest and belly, tilting his head at a painful angle, feeling the coarse surface of the sandstone rasping his cheek, no doubt scraping away his skin. Tears came to his eyes as his nose was momentarily squashed and his chest felt like his horse was standing on it, then – he stumbled.

God almighty! He made it! He was in the underground cell block and the prisoners were all yelling at him, coughing in the smoke and. . . .

He stumbled through, bleeding hands slapping his pockets for the set of keys and hoping like hell they were the right ones.

'Jake!' he yelled, eyes still getting used to the dimness: he could hear the flames roaring above.

'Here!' Just the single word: all that was needed.

Jake was in the middle cell. The other two prisoners, one either side of Jake, were reaching through the bars now, hands beckoning, cracked voices urging Brock to set them all free.

Brock didn't waste time: he had Jake – very shaky and bearing signs of a beating – clinging to his left arm. He literally dragged the younger man out of the cell, almost deafened by the urgent bawling of the other two men.

He glanced at them but they were no more than dark shapes, and tossed the keys into the nearest cell.

As the third man yelled at the others trying to find the keys in the darkness of the cell floor, Brock half-carried, half-dragged Jake to the third boulder.

His heart stopped! He was sure it stopped! Because the damn boulder wasn't moving. He pushed and nudged, got a leg up and tried to straighten it for leverage but the big rock stayed put, trapping them all.

'What's wrong?' Jake gasped, clinging tightly to Brock's arm.

'Damn boulder tilted just enough to let me in, now

it won't damn well budge! And if it don't, you're gonna have company in these damn cells – *me*!'

'Tr-try *pullin'* instead – of – *pushin'*. . . .'

Brock knew then that was the answer: push from the outside, pull to tilt it from the inside.

The other two prisoners were still squabbling over something as Brock felt the boulder finally move and he pushed Jake through the tight gap, wriggled and scraped to get through himself into the comparative cool of the night now shot through with rolling clouds of choking smoke.

The crowds were now mostly on the far side of the upper block where the flames roared and climbed ten feet high.

Brock stumbled to where he had stashed the two horses, Jake breathing hard, sagging against him, impeding his progress.

'They work you over, kid?'

'Some sonuver with a big, black moustache.'

'Don't worry about him now. Come on. No time for talk,' Brock grunted and boosted Jake into the saddle. Jake sagged over the saddlehorn as Brock mounted his impatient black.

'Grab that horn and hang on, kid! We're about to break some records for gettin' up into them hills.'

Before they cleared the area, the fire flared up and threw flickering light over them.

The gathered mob, fire-fighters and those simply there to gawk, stared in surprise as the horses lunged away through what had become a hellish night.

A couple of guns barked desultorily but neither

looked back as they ran their mounts into the smoke for cover.

Brock wondered how long their freedom would last? Bronson would send a mighty big posse after them and no doubt would put a price on their head big enough to make it worthwhile trying to collect.

CHAPTER 17

HOW DID HE DIE?

Sheriff Carl Bronson knew he had seriously underestimated Brock Chase. He had wanted to entice Brock to come in and attempt to rescue Jake Cash, but damned if he had reckoned on the man being successful!

Bronson had figured it would be futile, and he, with a few carefully chosen men, would be able to nail both Brock and Jake.

Shot and killed while trying to escape!

It had a mighty good ring to it, and would look good in the newspaper article he envisaged about himself pitting his wits against these professional renegades.

He would be set for life: feted for his own courage and foresight. There would be no doubt he would once again be elected sheriff of Storm County and able to retire in a few years with a lifetime pension.

'Yeah! I thank you Brock Chase, and that snotty-nosed Jake Cash, too! Welcome any time, you sons of bitches! Just don't expect to live very long!'

There was no problem in getting a posse together. Somehow word got around that the pair had a large price on their head for crimes in the past, committed in several distant counties and states, mostly hinted at, but with enough blurred details to make them sound like dangerous killers who ought not be allowed to stay on the loose any longer than necessary.

'I can get access to these rewards,' Bronson assured the men, when he was getting his posse together. 'Most are payable anywhere in the United States where Chase is arrested or – preferably, I hear on the quiet – shot down like the menace to honest citizens he is. Not sure about the kid, but, well, he's his sidekick, ain't he?'

Not everyone believed these tales, of course, but as the lies spread and attractive-sounding reward figures were bandied about, it seemed that more than half the blamed town was eager to join the posse.

'Aw, now, folks,' Bronson said, trying to look really worried. 'I'd sure like to give you *all* a crack at these bounties but – you know me. *Get the job done, quick an' clean.* Don't like to waste County funds, but I try to be fair about such things, so— Look: we've got two desperate men on the run. Two.' He swept an arm around and grinned. '*Two!*' he said again. 'And what else we got here? Twenty men, at least. Well, I reckon these rannies ain't *that* dangerous! so, I'll take ten men— Now just lemme finish! *Ten* men. We'll go after Brock and the kid for half a day!'

There was silence as the group waited for more details. 'Yeah, half a day. We don't get some definite sign, OK, we go ahead and follow anyway, but – *but* we don't cut no *real* sign, then that posse comes back to town and I take *another* ten men and pick up where we left off. If we can keep doin' that, we'll run 'em down. But *amigos*, we keep to the time limits, keep changin' the posse, an' I reckon it'll be fair if the reward is split between the group that actually does run 'em to ground.'

There were plenty of arguments for and against that idea, but Bronson remained adamant and eventually, grudgingly, it was agreed.

'We keep up the pressure, don't let 'em rest, or get any sleep, don't give 'em a chance to get fresh hosses, decent grub, or any more ammunition.' He beamed around at the somewhat bedazzled would-be possemen.

'An' don' forget, it's murder now that Chip Lang's dead. He weren't no great citizen, Old Chip, but, by hell, I don't aim to let Chase, nor anyone else, get away with murder, not in my bailiwick! So we get after 'em an' see to it they don't stand a goddamn chance!' he finished, and there was even a half-hearted cheer from his audience.

Louisa stopped in her tracks, halfway across the street, causing a minor mix-up of swearing riders and the wagons and buckboard traffic.

'Hey, lady,' a stubbled man in a buckboard yelled. 'Quit dreamin'! I nearly run you down then!'

'Oh, I-I'm sorry, Mr Crane. It's just that I hadn't seen that Wanted notice before.' She indicated a dodger nailed to the corner post of the stage station, the ink still wet and glistening.

It read: WANTED FOR MURDER and Brock Chase and Jake Cash were named as the fugitives.

She turned and saw the sheriff on the boardwalk tacking up a similar notice on another corner post. Mouth set rather grimly, she strode across.

'Sheriff! What – what's this about murder? Brock and Jake? There must be some mistake.'

The lawman touched a hand to his hatbrim. 'Sorry, Lou, it's true. Chip Lang died from those head injuries. He got 'em in a fight with Chase an' that makes it murder in my book.'

'But Doc Beecham said Chip's injuries weren't fatal. He told me that when I brought them to his notice. He said that Chip didn't have a fractured skull as was first thought, but he did have a serious concussion, but it was not necessarily fatal.'

'I ain't no sawbones, Louisa,' cut in the lawman, tersely. 'Doc said Lang's dead from his injuries and that's good enough for me. This damn Chase has been runnin' wild an' I've had a bellyful, so I've put out a dodger on him. I ain't said wanted "Dead or Alive" but I gotta admit I'm tempted.'

She said nothing, but whirled and stomped along the boardwalk to Doc Beecham's office half a block down.

The old short-sighted medic squinted at her, opened his mouth to speak, but Louisa didn't give him a chance.

'You told me Chip Lang's injuries weren't fatal!'

'And I stand by that,' Beecham said, in a phlegmy voice, obviously annoyed at the interruption. 'Lang's skull was not fractured as I first thought, but he did have concussion – not, in my opinion, serious enough to cause his death, but—' He shrugged. 'It wouldn't be the first time I've mistaken a diagnosis, Louisa. In fact, I'm thinking of retiring at the end of the year.'

'Well, that will be the town's loss, Doctor, but this charge of murder! It's – it's ridiculous!'

The old medic ran a hand over his sparse grey hair and looked uneasy. 'I've said I sometimes make mistakes. I'm afraid ours is not yet an exact science, but—' He paused, looking at her now with his rheumy eyes, 'This must not go beyond these walls, Louisa. Will you give me your word?'

Startled, the girl nodded, not sure she could speak right away.

'I think Chip was murdered— No,wait! I didn't accuse your friend Brock Chase! But I've examined Chip and I think a head injury did, in fact, cause his death.'

'But you just said—'

'And you heard me! Lang was suffering concussion. He did not have a skull fracture. But he did have a fresh bruise on the back of his head, low down at the base of the neck. It caused bleeding within the skull and in the brain which is what killed him.'

She was frowning. 'A *new* wound?'

He nodded. 'I have no idea how he came by it, but it was done with something solid and heavy. Perhaps – yes, perhaps like a gun butt, or an empty whiskey bottle.'

Her hand went to her mouth. 'My God! Who. . . ?'

He looked at her steadily. 'I have no idea. Only that

it was done after I had seen him and while he was in the rear room of the law office, waiting to be moved to the infirmary. I believe he was alive then, tho' quite poorly. I – er – believe it's the law's responsibility now. I do not wish to involve myself further.'

She was momentarily speechless, but, as she started to speak, he held up a wrinkled hand and turned to his desk, pulling some handwritten papers towards him.

'Now, I'm very busy, Louisa, I cannot spare you any more time, not even one more minute. So I must bid you farewell, at least for now.'

'But, now you suspect—?'

He didn't even glance up. Too busy, or *too reluctant* to get more deeply involved.

She left, still in a partial daze.

Someone had seen an opportunity to get rid of Brock Chase and maybe Jake Cash, too.

And they had murdered Chip Lang to do it.

She couldn't just stand by and see two innocent men blamed for a murder they didn't commit no matter what she had promised Doc Beecham.

But she would have to go carefully, very, very carefully.

The real murderer was still on the loose.

Having killed once, there was absolutely no reason to think he would hesitate to kill again if he believed he was going to be exposed.

CHAPTER 18

LONG RUN TO FREEDOM

Brock Chase knew this country.

This was land he had checked out many times before deciding to sign-on for prove-up in the area he had eventually chosen.

Although Jake's spread was next door – and they actually overlapped according to the rough maps drawn by the Lands Department – Jake had not ventured very far into the hills. Brock had shown him some small, hidden valleys that had meagre supplies of water, and therefore graze, but which could be used in times of drought.

He was surprised that Brock did not make for one of these valleys now, urged his sweating mount up alongside.

'How about one of them places you showed me? The

valleys we were gonna use if there was no rain, and—'

'Don't want to give away their location, kid.'

'But no one else knows about 'em.'

'And that's the way I want it to be.'

'Hell! You don't really figure we're ever gonna be allowed to settle in hereabouts again, do you?'

'Don't trust Bronson and his crew is all. If we go hide in one of them places, he'll bring in Indian trackers and they'll flush us for sure.'

'Ye-ah – could be. But where else do we go? I mean we got the law on our tails now. Crooked or not, Bronson is a duly-elected lawman and he can call in the whole damn County to help him. Someone's bound to flush us.'

'Then might be best if we go away for a spell.'

Jake all but hauled rein, then abruptly slowed his mount, breaking its rhythmic stride. He was busy for a short time, before spurring up alongside Brock again.

'Brock, must be the wind in my ears. Thought you said you was thinkin' of hightailin' it away from here?'

'It's an option.'

'Like hell! I ain't leavin' what I busted a gut to build! Not for the likes of Bronson or—'

'I said only that it's an option – a temporary one.'

Jake was quiet for a few seconds, and Brock lifted an arm, pointed left and up at what everyone around here had regarded as near a solid wall of growing timber as ever existed.

'Wh—? Not up there! Christ, man, we'd be a week tryin' to find a way in, and as for gettin' *out*!'

His words slowed as he watched Brock shake his

head slowly and definitely.

'Told you, I always try to find a back door – *several's* better. There'll be a way in there.'

Jake blew out his cheeks, made a 'Go for your life' gesture with his hands, or maybe an 'I give up!' one.

Damned if he could keep up with this ranny who called himself Brock Chase. But he sure had a tight grip on survival, so Jake was quite willing to follow his lead.

And Brock Chase did lead him into that near-impenetrable wall of tangled timber and thorny brush.

'How in hell did you find such a way in here? I reckon a man on foot would think twice about even tryin', and here we are in a small clearin' – even with some goddamn *flowers*, just patches where the sun manages to get through.'

'I looked around a mite before decidin' on that prove-up block.'

Jake stared hard, but Brock would not turn his head and look at him. 'By hell! You *must* be on the dodge real bad.'

'Said I might tell you about it someday.'

'You don't reckon – that's mebbe – today? Seein' as we're in this together. . . ?'

They dismounted in the cramped clearing and Jake's horse wasn't happy with the lack of space. He had to take time to get it calmed down.

Brock just stood holding short rein on his black, stroking its neck absently, the horse motionless.

'You got him trained mighty good,' Jake commented.

'Had to work at it, but, yeah, he's a good pard. We

been some places to make your hair stand on end. Jake, my problems are *mine*, I'm dodgin' something that happened a long time ago, and a long, long way from here.'

'Yeah, your accent says you're from a long ways South.'

Brock's eyes narrowed slightly. 'Need to work on that a little more, I guess. Leave it set, Jake. Here an' now is what we ought to be talking about.'

Jake's lips tightened but then he nodded. 'OK. I – er – guess you're right. Anyway, I'm obliged to you for savin' my neck, so, you just wanna leave it like that, pard?'

He thrust out his right hand tentatively. Brock took it without hesitation. 'See? I *did* train you well.'

Jake smiled crookedly. 'Don't mean I still ain't curious.'

'They say it killed the cat . . . curiosity. But I ain't partial to cats, anyway.'

'See I've got some trainin' to do with you then.'

'Let's leave it till we get outa here and over this damn mountain.'

Which was no easy chore.

As darkness began to fill the stand of close-packed trees with solid black shadows, the mounts grew restless. But there was enough grass amongst the trees for them to nibble at, Jake watching over them first, then Brock.

They heard the posse mostly, though they glimpsed them twice and Jake whistled softly.

'Judas! There's at least a dozen of 'em! An' I think mebbe another bunch a little westward, back toward

151

town. Lucky for us they ain't even considerin' this place.'

'They could get round to it. Bronson ain't too sharp, but he's stubborn and he's gettin' desperate. That's when he'll decide to check this place out.'

Jake looked around him in alarm. 'Hell! Take a deal of gettin' outa here! Look what it took us to get in!'

'We just gotta hope Bronson decides like everyone else it can't be done – and *wouldn't* be by a couple of fools on the run.'

Jake nodded and they were silent for a time, the horses keeping them busy, growing more restless and uneasy.

'We go after dark?' Jake asked, keeping his voice low.

'Before.'

'Huh! Look, this slope faces west, we'll have the glow of sundown on it for at least a half-hour, mebbe longer'

'You don't reckon going then would be wise?'

'Hell, no! No one in his right mind would try to clear this place with the sundown on it.'

He said this slowly, squinting now at Brock.

'Son of a gun! I just said it, didn't I? No one would think any fool would try to move before dark.'

'It'll be risky,' Brock warned. 'We'll have to use the shadows, lead the horses – or leave 'em.'

'Hell! I don't like that.'

'Give it some thought: chance a bullet and maybe your horse bein' shot out from under you, or be sneaky and crawl out on our bellies.'

'Like a coupla snakes. And likely put our hands on a couple. Hell, Brock, maybe we just better stay put.'

152

'That's the other option. It's chancy, but I reckon we could pull it off.'

Jake was silent briefly, then said, 'If we do. . . ? I say *if.*'

'If they think we're holed-up in here, what would you do in Bronson's place?'

Jake thought, then swore softly. 'I-I reckon I'd flush us by settin' fire to these trees. *Goddamn*, Brock! He'll do it, too! Bronson will burn us out!'

Brock looked at him hard.

'Or we could beat him to it,' he said quietly.

'W-what?' Jake paused, frowning. '*We* do the burnin', that what you're sayin'?'

'It's an idea.'

'Yeah, but—! Well, I reckon we could likely *do* it, but again, where's the advantage?'

'It'd get us outa here and we could make our run for it.'

'But where? I don't wanta lose what land I've got.'

'But have we got our land, Jake? It's not certain, not if Bronson and McBarr keep out them Wanted notices on us. Fact, they've already done a mighty big heap of harm: they've made us outlaws, *wanted men*. Now we can't ever qualify for prove-up, so we'll be barred from holdin' any land that was set aside for Veterans and the like.'

'All right! We move out, go someplace else, change our names an'— Uh-oh! You've already changed yours!'

Brock smiled slightly. 'One of those things you can do again – and again – just about any time you like.'

153

Jake was frowning deeply now. 'Would you go through all that again?'

Brock's crooked smile widened slightly.

'Let's say I'm used to it, Jake.'

It was not an easy decision.

Where would they go? Where could they go, for that matter?

Bronson was one hard character and he had hard men on his payroll who knew how to use their guns.

The thing was, neither Brock nor Jake knew what Bronson was after. Oh, sure, the rumoured gold was always in the background, but, when you got right down to it, that's all it was: a rumour. No one had found any real traces of that missing bullion. You could hardly count the small nugget Brock had found and that had triggered the whole damn thing. There was a lot of wishful thinking behind *that*.

Now, none of it was relevant, not for Brock or Jake, because they had been outlawed by a sheriff who only needed his badge to back up his claim that they had broken the law, and so were finished as prove-up contenders and could never qualify again – unless the legal charges were disproved or withdrawn.

But, if they didn't do something. . . .

'How trustworthy is that so-called legend about the gold being buried in the landslide on the land we've been working?' Brock asked suddenly, but quietly.

Jake snapped his head up: he looked kind of haggard and worn-down, Brock thought and wondered what *he* looked like, but to hell with looks.

If they found the gold they could look just about any way they liked: go to a barber regularly, wear decent clothes, even take neck-deep baths with soap froth tickling their nostrils. They could live it up!

But this was getting out of hand. Dreaming got you nowhere in a deal like this. *Doing* was the thing. As long as you knew what you were doing.

'It's gospel enough for Bronson and McBarr to keep us in their sights, Brock. I wouldn't like to bet my last dollar on it, but there's something about our land that's got a lot of folk interested, we know that. Tie it in to the legend – well, it could make sense, huh?'

He shrugged and let it lie at that.

It was good enough for Brock Chase to say, 'Let's tie it in then and try to undo the knot.' He looked steadily at Jake. 'What we got to lose?'

Jake gave him a steady look. 'Me, I want to know what we got to *gain*!'

'That's easy, we'll be rich.'

'Or dead.'

'Not an option, *amigo*, not an option.'

CHAPTER 19

KEEP RUNNING

They both knew that Bronson wouldn't leave them be. That was a foregone conclusion. The man was on his run now, reaching with both hands. Anyone who was stupid enough to get in his way was a candidate for Boot Hill.

'We're gonna *have* to stay here all night,' Brock said levelly. 'I'll take first watch.'

'I'm not much more'n a kid, Brock, but I'm tough enough to do my stint. I was under age, but I lied an' did my bit in the War, mister. You know what that means?'

'Got some kinda hazy notion about it,' Brock admitted slowly and with a light touch to his words. 'But I'll still take first watch – an' don't take offence. It's nothing to do with your age or how you grew up, it's me. I've got a crushing ache in my right knee, won't let me sleep, anyway. Old war wound actin'-up.'

'Noticed you limpin' a mite, didn't want to mention it. Fact, thought it was just a touch of . . . old age . . . creepin' in.'

Brock gave him a steady look. 'Too bad you ain't gonna be able to find out for yourself – what old age is like, I mean!'

Jake grinned. 'Sorry! Din' mean to ruffle your feathers. They look a leetle bit grey in the dark!'

'By hell! You *are* gonna die young! You might make a good-lookin' corpse, though. Mebbe that's some compensation.'

Jake was starting to laugh when there was a gunshot from beside a boulder. The flash briefly illuminated the shooter already on the move to different cover as Jake spun violently, grasping high somewhere in the chest area before he crashed to the ground.

Brock Chase was already down, stretched out, his six gun in his hand, elbow digging firmly into the ground. The foresight was just visible in the rapidly fading light. There was movement behind some low rocks close to the boulder, which told him that the shooter must be lying full-length because they lacked the height to give a crouching man enough cover.

Brock triggered twice.

There was a violent movement of a rearing, tumbling shape and a man staggered half-upright, fighting to bring up the six-gun he held at waist level.

Brock shot him again and this time he went down hard, slid on to his side, neck bent at a sharp angle against the rock where he had fallen.

Then several shots rang across the golden slopes and

Brock dropped flat, trying to force his long, lean body into the ground.

He felt his hat whipped off his head, his hair flying upwards briefly and then the wild, savage sound of a ricochet, inches from his ear.

'Jake! Jake!' Brock called, not taking his eyes off the man he had shot, but the man had given a series of trembling shudders and now lay still – *very* still.

'Where you hit, boy?'

'Just skimmed my shoulder muscle.' Jake's voice sounded strong, but Brock could tell he was biting back against pain. 'Ain't bleedin' much – hell!'

He dropped flat as another gun, angled off to his left where there was a ragged line of rocks, spoke rapidly. Brock reared back as sand kicked into his face, stung his eyes. He dropped back into the shallow trench where he had been lying.

The snarl of ricochets made him wince and clasp his hands instinctively over his head.

That had been a rifle – no! A *carbine*, by the sound of it, the shorter barrel making a distinctive, flat *cough* as the weapon fired.

Brock's rifle was out of reach so he was just going to have to use his six-gun – not really effective at this range against a long gun or even a *short* long gun like a carbine.

'That's McBarr,' grated Jake quietly. 'He stole that carbine from Charley Reardon. Muzzle got banged up when he fell in the rocks runnin' away. It's always made that kinda *sneezin'* sound . . . like a man with a cold.'

'Then it's time it took somethin' for it.'

158

Brock was on the move and Jake marvelled once more how little noise the big rancher made. But *there he was*! Just another creeping shadow, as the sun sank, dozens of other shadows changing shape now.

Then one reared up, about the height of a man on his knees. Jake gaped at a sudden blur of speed where Brock crouched, saw the six-gun come up even as a rifle swung towards him. Brock dropped flat, Colt held in both hands now. The gun bucked violently against his thumb and wrist as he fired three rapid, equally-spaced shots.

The shadowy man over there jerked and jumped briefly, like a puppet with suddenly severed strings, then fell with a dull crash.

'Gawd, Brock!' Jake said, loud enough for Brock to hear the shock behind the word. 'That was the god-damned sheriff you just shot!'

Brock turned his smoking Colt this way and that. 'Funny thing: this damn gun never did like lawmen.'

Jake's eyebrows arched and he said in a voice that just shook a little, 'I don't s'pose I better ask any questions about that!'

Brock smiled thinly. 'Might be best if you don't. *Goddammit*! Gonna be hard to explain this away, though: shootin' down a lawman, good or bad. Once they pin on that damn badge—' He shook his head slowly. 'Don't like this. Three times it's happened now – none of 'em worth a hill of beans, but – *but*! The sons of bitches wore badges so that makes 'em like goddamn saints.'

He glared and Jake reared back a shade at the

159

disturbing look. He pressed the neckcloth more firmly into his bullet graze.

'You – you're on the run again, then?' he said flatly.

'*Again?* Hell, I've been on the run for years for *accidentally* killin' a crooked marshal in – well, don't matter where. *Now* I've just nailed another. Looks like the reward goes up. I'll have every bounty hunter from here to Canada looking for me.'

Jake looked at him steadily for a long minute, then said, 'You can always change your name.'

For a moment he thought he had misjudged Brock's sense of humour and then the right-hand corner of the man's mouth twitched.

'Yeah, I could always do that – again!'

'New name – new background. Hey! Maybe we could pass for brothers – you the oldest of course!'

Brock frowned again. 'Mebbe I could pass as your *father*. Then I could tell everyone about the sassy, *illegitimate* son I'm stuck with!'

Jake grinned. 'You got a real nice way of putting things, you know that? Pappy!'